William Henry Suttor

Australian stories retold and sketches of country life

William Henry Suttor

Australian stories retold and sketches of country life

ISBN/EAN: 9783744750813

Printed in Europe, USA, Canada, Australia, Japan

Cover: Foto ©Andreas Hilbeck / pixelio.de

More available books at **www.hansebooks.com**

Australian

STORIES RETOLD

AND

Sketches of Country Life.

BY W. H. SUTTOR, M.L.C.,

NEW SOUTH WALES.

Bathurst :
GLYNDWR WHALAN, HOWICK STREET.
1887.

To the Memory

OF

MY MUCH-LOVED AUSTRALIAN FATHER,

Who for twenty-eight years of his life was a member of our Representative Parliaments, commencing with the very first, and was always a patriotic, energetic, and unselfish worker, and who, although born under the Southern Cross, was ever a true-hearted Englishman,

I DEDICATE

THIS LITTLE VOLUME,

which, in a large part, contains a record of my filial service for him.

PREFACE.

ACTING in accordance with the unexpected, and therefore flattering, solicitations of many friends, I have consented to collect in a small volume the " Stories" and " Country Sketches" contained herein. Originally written for a charitable purpose, and published in the *Daily Telegraph* in Sydney, they have beguiled many weary hours of their author at a time of much anxiety for all those who, like himself, were interested in the great pastoral industry of the country. I am no judge of their merits, if, indeed, they have any. The first person who suggested their collection in this form was the late Chief Justice, Sir James Martin, who was pleased to speak in terms somewhat too laudatory of them, and in his rapid manner said, " You must put them in a book, you know—you must put them in a book." Well, here they are in a book. There is little or nothing imaginative in the volume. The " Stories Retold" are chiefly gathered from the Press records of the day, and from the word of mouth of old colonial friends who have some recollection of the events narrated. The " Sketches of Country Life" are derived almost wholly from my own experiences. The descriptions of men and scenery are exactly set down as they appeared to me. So many wonderful changes have taken place in colonial society since " I was young," that I venture to hope the book may not prove uninteresting to those who have not been eyewitnesses of those changes.

CONTENTS.

AUSTRALIAN STORIES RETOLD—

SKETCHES OF COUNTRY LIFE—

SKETCHES OF COUNTRY LIFE—

Australian Stories Retold.

MY GRANDFATHER'S POCKETBOOK.

IT is with much reverence I take up this old book and pry into its contents. It is a large book of its kind, and I have not yet seen a coat pocket that would hold it comfortably. It measures exactly seven inches in length by five inches in breadth, and has a girth when empty of nearly one foot. Old age and venerableness are stamped indelibly upon its smoothed and well-worn old skin. Although, babe and man, I have been a colonist for over fifty years, I feel that I am one of the veriest of new chums in its ancient presence. It belongs indisputably to the eighteenth century — the French Revolution, Napoleon, Nelson, Wellington, Trafalgar, Waterloo: it has been an inanimate witness of all the stirring times these names recall. It has long survived Emperors, Kings, and great ones of the earth, and has not yet lost all usefulness. Old letters and papers it has held for near a century it still enfolds in secure and loving embrace. It has been the unconscious recipient of many hopes and fears. It is identified with the early struggles and hard times of colonial life. Let us examine some of its contents. They are suggestive of much that is interesting in our history. The first paper we take out is a letter dated February 3, 1800, written more than 87 years ago. The paper is of good texture, and is gilt-edged. The writer, Sir Joseph Banks, sailed into Botany Bay with Captain Cook. He took a keen interest in the early settlement of these lands ; indeed, it was largely through his representations and influence that the Government were induced to colonize Australia. The letter has reference to the misdoings of a Gosport waggoner, who neglected to deliver some grape vines at their proper destination into the care of the recipient of the letter, and has thereby kindled the wrath of Sir Joseph. These vines, with many other useful plants, were intended to be carried to Sydney in charge of the owner of our pocketbook, a young man of six and twenty years, whose imagination had been much stirred by accounts of this distant land, and who had energy and ambition enough to desire to seek a larger field for his industry than the old country seemed to afford. The outward appearance of the letter claims some little attention. Our fathers of that date knew nothing of the convenient gummed envelope. The paper is doubled down from top to bottom, so that the two edges meet in the centre. The two other edges are then folded down ; one edge is pushed into the folds of the other ; a paste wafer is used to stick the two together. The direction written upon it tells of an old privilege once held by members of Parliament. In the left corner is the name of one " Steph. Cottrell." This signature has had the effect of authorising the post-office to carry the letter free of charge to its destination. The next letter (from the same writer) is dated August 10, 1802, and is addressed to New

South Wales. Many pertinent inquiries are made as to the kinds of fruit and grain-bearing and other useful plants that may be thought suitable to the soil and climate of the colony.. It is advised that the capsicum should be planted, "as it might be beneficial to Governor King's constitution." The feeding of this early and somewhat irascible Governor on this extremely pungent fruit is a curious suggeston. I am not aware whether or not the idea was carried out. Between the times of the writing of these two letters our pocketbook has been carried a long voyage. In the month of October, 1798, it had been taken on board H.M.S. Porpoise, and had gone as far as Spithead, when the exigencies of the war with France prevented further voyaging. In the month of September, 1799, after eleven months of delay, a fresh start was made with a large convoy of sail, with twenty ships of war, under the command of Admiral Sir Roger Curtis, a magnificent sight, which filled the heart of our intending colonist with pride at the power of his country. However, a gale coming on, the Porpoise was disabled and returned to Spithead, where our voyagers had to remain until a vessel, La Infanta Amelia, and lately taken from the Spaniards, to be called the Porpose, was refitted; so that it was not till the 17th March, 1800, that final departure for Australia was made. After a long delay at the Cape of Good Hope, the owner of our book, with his family, at length entered Sydney Heads on November 6th, 1800, and saw " with admiration the many coves and headlands of Port Jackson, its deep waters and secure anchorages; the wooded heights, the bluff heads, the rude rocks which presented to the view innumerable primitive and romantic scenes, which cultivation had done nothing to reclaim." They also noticed " several bark canoes (a novel sight) of the natives with women in them fishing, a convict ship from Ireland, and a ship

from India. Two small wharves were observed, one called
the King's and the other the Governor's, on opposite sides
of the cove.   Campbell's Wharf was then being erected.
Sydney was more like a camp than a town.   The streets
were full of stumps and dead trees, the houses were all
covered with thatch, the walls chiefly of wattle and dab
whitewashed.   A few had glazed windows.   In Pitt and
George streets some weatherboard houses were to be
seen."   On the day after his arrival our colonist waited
upon Governor King, who, he thought, received him
with ill humour, and advised him "not to think of
staying at Sydney, as every man there was a rogue, and
they would be surely robbed of all they possessed ; to
remain on board till a house could be got at Parramatta;
not to trust anybody ;" and further, "that he could not
be troubled with his affairs ; he had six thousand people
to govern, and that was as much as he could do."
Rather a disheartening prospect for a new chum this ; all
the more so, as before leaving England he had been led to
expect some consideration from the Governor.   Perhaps
it was this scene duly related to Sir J. Banks that sug-
gested the capsicum diet.   However, he followed the
Governor's advice, and managed to secure a two-
roomed cottage at the then rural village of Parramatta,
to which place he had made a walking excursion.
Having found there an old friend in Mr. George Caley,
the botanist, and made the acquaintance of the Rev. S.
Marsden, and of Mr. Lewin, painter and ornithologist,
and of a Dr. Thompson, all of whom assisted him in the
search for a piece of land to take up as his grant, things
began to look somewhat brighter.   Parramatta in 1800
was but a small nucleus of a town, and consisted principally of prisoners' huts.   Having found a fertile spot,
the Government built for our new arrival a small cottage, and allowed a certain number of prisoners to clear
some of the land ;   and, in about eighteen months after,

he had the supreme satisfaction of " settling " upon his own farm, and of harvesting his first crop of corn or maize. There was much destitution and even starvation in the colony in those days, caused by frequent and devastating floods in the Hawkesbury, which, covering the cultivated land, destroyed the crops.

The next letters we examine were written by our colonist himself, and are addressed to his wife from the Sydney Gaol, 180-9. New and strange experience had come upon him. Governor Bligh had been deposed by the military, and was an exile from his seat of Government. He was an eye witness of the event of that memorable evening of January 26, 1808, having from curiosity followed the troops to the gates of the Governor's residence. How he came in contact with the rebel Government is not very clear; but certain it is he was ordered to do something which drew from him a certain letter " with contumelious expressions;" for which writing, and for refusing to plead to his indictment for such conduct, he was cast into gaol for the period of six months, always hoping for a day when the " king would enjoy his own again," when his friend Governor Bligh would be reinstated.

The next paper is a tiny, dainty, delicate gilt-edged note, written in characters of almost microscopic smallness, but are of perfect form, and are as clear and as legible as a schoolboy's round text. A thoroughbred hand is manifest in every line of it, written by a lady seventy-five years ago, whose name is connected with the history of the colony. I fancy I can detect in the writing itself, where " I marked the particular turn of her Ps and Qs," evidences of that firm bravery and filial loving duty that prompted Mrs. Putland (Bligh's daughter) to defy the rude soldiers, and one would fain hope, almost shame those into submission who came to depose her father. The letter is kind, short, practical, and to the purpose.

" Mrs. O'Connell" (she was then the wife of Colonel, afterwards Sir Maurice O'Connell), " was hoping to have the pleasure of informing Mrs. Suttor that Captain Bodie of the late ship from England, saw the Hindostan, Dromedary, and Porpoise going into Rio on the 25th July (1810), as he was coming out of that port, but unfortunately did not speak to them. The Colonel (O'Connell) requests Mrs. S, will mention what description of workmen she wants, and when she will be ready to receive them, as he forgets. The Governor (Macquarie) will be at Parramatta next week, and the Colonel wishes Mrs. S. then to speak to him about exchanging her bullock."

This letter was written to assure her friend, Mrs. S., that, so far as was known, her husband, who had gone to England with Bligh to give evidence in his case, was so far safe. This witness, to the day of his death, fifty years after, was a firm believer in the honesty of purpose of Bligh. He had, as we have seen, given strong evidence of this belief in preferring to be cast into prison rather than forsake his friend and acknowledge as lawful rulers persons whom he believed and knew to be rebels, for their own selfish and not patriotic purposes. He always spoke of him as a firm and kind-hearted English gentleman, and no tyrant and no coward, and that his single purpose was to prevent the wholesale demoralization of the people of the colony through the rum-selling propensities of people in high places. It has always been the fashion to speak of Bligh as a tyrant, because of the unfortunate mutiny of a part of his crew on board the Bounty. The subsequent history of these mutineers affords a clue to the reason for their insubordination. Having secured the ship, they went back to the seductions of Tahiti. They sailed from there, taking with them a number of Tahitian women and a few men. They beached the ship on Pitcairn's Island. When discovered in 1808 only one (Smith or Adams) of the mutineers survived. Of Christian, the ringleader, two stories are told. One that he became insane and threw himself into the sea shortly after the landing at Pitcairn's. The other, that he, " for the short time he was spared, sullen and morose, committed many acts of wanton oppression," and with the rest was murdered by their Tahitian men slaves. If the first be true, then is it too much to suppose that the mutiny was, in a great measure, due to the incipient mania of Christian ? If the latter, then it shows what a tyrannical, insane temper this man had, whose harshness could goad the gentle and timorous Tahitian to such an outbreak and just retribution. The romantic story of the descendants of the mutineers has helped to veil the misdeeds of their forefathers, and to cloud unjustly the meritorious memory of Bligh. If Bligh were such a tyrant and coward, it is impossible to understand the implicit obedience of the men, his fellow-sufferers, cast adrift with him in the open boat at the time of the mutiny, during the most memorable voyage of the kind ever undertaken. Bligh's deposers accused him of cowardice after they deposed him, forgetting what a compliment they paid to his courage in marching nearly the whole regiment down to his house to seize him, knowing, too, as they did, that the lieutenant on guard would not resist his superior officer, the colonel. Men who used so much force to capture a single unarmed man were not competent judges to distinguish bravery from cowardice. To compare small things with great, the scene at Government House with our fair correspondent recalls Burke's famous and glowing words in reference to Marie Antoinette. One of the soldiers made a low and insulting remark to her. To the lasting shame of the officers, who were supposed to be high-minded English gentlemen, he was not rebuked by them. But the days of chivalry were past, those who could do battle for the noble cause of rum mono-poly were not likely to be touched by beauty in distress when "the craft was in danger."

While the owner of our book was away on this busi-ness, his wife was left, with her little children, to fight the battle of early colonial life as best she could. Not a word of repining from her. She "seen her duty a dead sure thing, and went for it there and then." A young girl, who, in 1798, married the man of her choice, and made the honeymoon trip a voyage to New South Wales, knowing that privation and hard work were at the end of it, was not likely to make a bad colonist. So, in the absence of her husband, she carries on the work of their little farm ; applies, as we see, to the Government for more workmen ; makes bargains for her stock ; and rules her convict servants with firmness and kind consi-deration. Many of those who, obtaining their freedom, lived and died in the service of her sons, always spoke of her with reverent affection. On his return, having been away more than two years, her husband finds the farm much improved. Her "counterfeit presentment" looks down upon me as I write. I know that the artist has, in drawing the large, calm, kind, and courageous eyes, and the firm lines about the mouth, faithfully de-picted her character. Hard struggle had this pair in those days ; but economy, plodding industry, and the gift to seize an opportunity, to "take the tide at the flood," brought in time comparative wealth and much happiness, and a long life crowned with "love, obedi-ence, troops of friends," made ample amends for many sore and rough trials.

The next paper is a triplicate order on the Treasury of England to pay Mr. ———, a very worthy servant, the sum of £25, his six months' salary, from June to.

December, 1816, not £1 per week. It must have been in some way negotiated by the owner of our book. This gentleman, through patient industry and making good use of honest opportunity, captured fortune and left descendants. I recollect once overhearing one of these speaking with much supercilious contempt of the social position of some who were then much higher up the ladder than was her grandfather when that order was made out. "Ah, my dear madam," thought I, "if you only knew what my grandfather's pocketbook reveals, you would, I am sure, add one more to your many perfections by showing a little more charity and kindly consideration to those who, with laudable and honest ambition, are striving (as your grandfather did) to leave their descendants in the position in which you now find yourself." But is it not the way of the world to despise those who occupy the places from which we flatter ourselves we have risen ? I once knew a man who, having attained wealth, never could conceal his contempt for what he was pleased to call persons of "low birth," himself being—well, never mind! he had nothing to boast of, as a living exemplification of the proverb, "It's a wise child that knows its own father."

Here are many letters from George Caley and Allan Cunningham, both men of science, doing much hard work to enlarge the sphere of botanical and geographical knowledge. Caley was among the first to try to scale the Blue Mountains, and managed to push his way as far as near Woodford, where a stone cairn on the old roadside, marking the spot of his furthest journeying, was called Caley's Repulse. Some of his letters are from England. One, dated 1812, gives an interesting account of the people near Manchester. He writes; "In these parts there has been a great deal of rioting, and, in short, throughout all the manufacturing counties, to the disgrace of the nation. These riots are said to originate from the high prices of provisions, decay of trade, and new inventions for facilitating labour, chiefly worked by steam engines. To see the factories that are in this country and the rapid manner of making goods, one would think there is more made than all the world could consume. Many of the people are out of employment, and numbers of parties can only get a bare subsistence. The middle class of people, I am told, have suffered and still do feel it most. If I may hazard a conjecture, I think England has manufactured too much. I saw hundreds going to attack a manufactory about two miles from here, and I must say they did not look like starved people. The chief beginners of the riots were colliers, who had no occasion to complain of the times, for steam engines furnished thousands of them with a livelihood. You may expect a fine lot of them perhaps by the receipt of this letter, and they will prove a different set from thieves, croppies, threshers, &c., &c. I should like to give some of them a good sweating in the New South Wales mountains." Some of these machine breakers were sent out here. An assigned servant of my father's was one of them. He used to tell an amusing story. The party of rioters he was with came to a church. Curiosity tempted them to look inside. They saw the organ, which, with its pipes, looked suspicious. "Wha'at be tha'at?" said one. "Woy, a zingin' (singing) masheen," was the reply. "A masheen, a singin' masheen," shouted the crowd." "Oh, dang un! let's smash un oop;" and smashed it accordingly was. Thus the right of the human voice to a complete monopoly of the utterances of sweet sounds was nobly vindicated. In this same letter he tells of the assassination of Percival by Bellingham. One part is to this effect: —"People would think New South Wales a fine place in reading the following paragraph, which I have copied from a paper:—'An elegant hospital has been

built by contract at Port Jackson. The condition on
which the building is reared is rather novel: 'That the
contractor should receive no money for the erection, but
should be permitted, in lieu thereof, to import 30,000
gallons of rum duty free.' "   This appears to have
been a stroke of genius. The hospital would, after this
importation, not be wanting in patients. The payment
for the building would ensure its usefulness.

As the population of the colony nine years after, when
the first census was taken, was under 30,000 persons,
this importation probably represented nearly two gallons
per head. At the present day, all spirits included, we
import about one gallon and a half per head per annum.
We always seem to have been good solid drinkers; the
droughty climate has much to answer for. Not long
since in Sydney, the president of a certain club at the
annual meeting, seeing from the balance-sheet that
affairs were very satisfactory, and judging of the true
cause, exclaimed as he pulled his venerable beard, "My
G—, gentlemen, we have drunk ourselves into a state of
prosperity."   History repeats itself, as the Treasurer's
annual statements renew the same story for the country.

One friend writes to tell of Napoleon's march to
Moscow; another of the return of Captain Parry's
expedition from the Arctic Seas; and among other
gossips relates " How Captain Parry's wife that was to
be on his return is on the point of marrying with someone else, and he likely to be out of his mind."   Luckily,
this last sad state of things did not happen, for Parry
came out here, and, living at Port Stephens, did good
service as a colonist in managing the affairs of the A.A.
Company.

A note from Dr. Lang, of date 1833, asking "for
views and opinions about the class of emigrants most
desirable for the colony, as he was going to England,
and may be able to make suggestions of value," is not

the least interesting of the budget.   There are letters from John Clark, an engraver, and father of Mrs. William Chambers.   From one of these I learn that so much of the proof sheets of the " Information for the People" as refer to Australia were submitted to our colonist, who was in Edinburgh at that time, for hints for revision, if need be, before final publication.   Some letters from Bligh himself are in the pocket-book, but as they throw no light upon the facts of the rebellion, they are, therefore, not quoted.

FISHER'S GHOST.

IN the year 1826 there lived at Campbelltown two persons who had been transported to New South Wales.   They were Frederick Fisher and George Worrall ; they were friends and lived together. Fisher owned a farm and some stock.   On the night of June 17, Fisher was in Campbelltown, and left a public-house there in company with other persons.   Some of these persons shortly afterwards came back to the inn and asked for Fisher, stating that they wanted to get money from him to purchase liquor.   Fisher was never after seen alive.   His disappearance gave rise to much remark, as his friend Worrall told people that he had left the colony to escape a prosecution for forgery and had sailed in a ship the name of which he gave. Worrall further stated that Fisher had authorised him in writing to deal with his property, and he offered for sale a horse and some timber known to belong to the supposed absconder. The written authority was never produced, but a document in reference to the horse was shown, and was at once seen to be a forgery by those who knew Fisher's signature. Worrall lost no time in going to Sydney to Mr. D. Cooper, to whom Fisher was in debt some £80, and offered to pay this debt provided the deeds of Fisher's farm, held by Cooper as security, were given up to him. This Cooper refused to do, and having questioned Worrall very closely about Fisher's disappearance, he suspected from Worrall's manner that Fisher had been made away with. Cooper had an intimate knowledge of Fisher, and was satisfied in his own mind that he had no reason for leaving the colony. The ship, too, in which Worrall said Fisher had sailed was not known to have been in Sydney Harbor. Cooper did not express his thoughts to Worrall but he did so to another person, who told Worrall of Cooper's suspicions, and observed his agitation when so told. In October (four months after Fisher's disappearance), the authorities thought it necessary to take some action. A reward was offered and Constable George Leeland was instructed to search for the body. He commenced the search at a spot about fifty rods from Worrall's place, and where some blood was found sprinkled on the rails of a fence. It was noticed that an attempt had been made to burn the fence at this spot, as though to destroy the blood marks. Two aboriginals joined in the search from this spot, and the party came to a waterhole in the creek Gilbert, one of the blacks, went into the water, and scumming off something from the surface with a maize leaf, smelt and tasted it, and said it was "white man's fat." Led by the natives, they went to another creek forty yards further, when one of the blacks struck an iron rod into the ground in a marshy spot and called out that there was something there. The place was dug, and the body of Fisher, not very much decomposed, was found. An inquest was held, and a verdict of wilful murder was found against some person or persons unknown. Worrall, a man named Laurence, and another, were apprehended. Worrall only was put upon his trial, and upon evidence wholly circumstantial, was convicted and executed. Early on the morning of his execution he confessed to the late Rev. W. Cowper that he had killed Fisher by misadventure; that he and Fisher were driving a horse from out of a crop of wheat; that he made a blow at the horse with a paling, and accidentally hit Fisher and killed him. As there were several wounds found on Fisher's head, this statement was also false. That he became alarmed lest he should be accused of murder, hid the body first in the reeds, and then where it was afterwards found. Such is the story as told, without any embellishment or hint of supernatural agency, in the *Sydney Gazette*, the *Monitor*, and the *Australian* of the first week in February, 1827. The *Monitor* contains some editorial comment, and remarks upon "the almost miraculous discovery four months after the murder had been committed." The words "almost miraculous" evidently referring only to the discovery after such a lapse of time. The story, which so far seems plain and simple enough, and not requiring much acumen to unravel, became celebrated for the assertion that a supernatural manifestation led to the discovery of the murderer.

It is stated that a man named Farley, leaving Campbelltown one night with probably some grog on board, having parted from his boon companions, returned to them, appearing in a frightened condition, with a statement that he had seen the ghost of Fisher at the slip-panel leading into the paddock at Fisher's house, and that the appearance pointed to the paddock. The ghost was dressed in the ordinary everyday garments of the

period, in fact, in Fisher's clothes. There can be no
doubt whatever that Fisher's body and clothes were at
this very time under the ground and rapidly becoming
in a very decomposed and unpresentable and (with
regard to the clothes especially) very rotten condition.
If the ghost really wore Fisher's clothes, one wonders
how such an unsubstantiality could support their weight,
unless, indeed (but this is too funny or too dreadful to
contemplate) clothes—material clothes—may become
sublimed and spiritualized, and be invested with a
future existence. (In this condition, will they wear
out?) But perhaps ghosts are able to wear clothes. I
once saw and heard the ghost of Hamlet's father in very
creaky boots; but I cannot say that their noisiness
added to the solemnity. It is a consolation to know, at
all events, that in spirit-land decency at least is strictly
preserved.

But may we not seek for a rationalistic theory to
account for this ghost? The ghost is not reported to
have been seen until four months had elapsed after the
time of the murder. It did not appear until those who
knew Fisher became perfectly satisfied that he did not
leave the colony, and that Worrall's statement about
him must have been untruthful. It is proved that the
night he was missed he left a public-house in company
with several persons. None of these seem to have
been called at the trial. It is most likely that
others knew of, if indeed they did not participate in, the
murder. What had been done had probably been
known to or discovered by Farley, and he then invented
the whole story to ease his conscience of a burden too
heavy to carry any longer. This gave a clue which,
when followed up, led to the finding of the body. The
neighbours, who were of the same class with Fisher and
Worrall, were not likely to have been deceived by Worrall's
lies. They were probably too loyal to one of their num-

ber to state openly what they knew. The blood on the fence, the attempt to burn it out, most surely was known to some of them. Other theories suggest themselves, but I venture to think that the above is most likely to be the correct one.

It has been suggested that the story of the ghost having been seen at all was a mythical growth of a later day. In contradiction to this idea, I have the authority of a correspondent who was intimately connected with the gentleman who had charge of the police in the district when the murder was done, to the effect that Farley's story did suggest the search for the body in the creek. But even so, this does not prove that Farley saw a ghost, but rather strengthens the solution given above. I am informed that the first time the story appeared in print, it was in an almanac published in the colony, and was written by a Mr. Kerr, who at or about the time was a tutor in the family of Mr. Howe, of Glenlee. It is shortly referred to in Montgomery Martin's book on the colonies, published in 1835. He evidently had implicit faith in the ghost, and writes of "the discovery of the murder as one of the inscrutible dispensations of Providence." In "Tegg's Monthly Annual" for March, 1836, the story is told with much imaginative detail, and evidently for the purpose of furnishing an interesting story rather than an ascer- tained matter of fact.

It is to be remarked that during the hearing of the case, the man who is said to have seen the ghost gave no evidence, nor is there any allusion whatever to any- thing supernatural having been supposed to have been manifested. It is also curious that the blacks should have led the party to the spot where the body was found. They are very observant, and most likely had previously seen marks and indications that, now a clue was given, they had no difficulty in following up.

VENGEANCE FOR IPPITHA.

N the latter part of the year 1838 there sat in the law offices in Sydney a tall, thin, bilious, sallow, and somewhat saturnine-looking man. His face was innocent of hair, and on his head he wore a jet-black wig. He was one of those men of whom one felt inquisitive at the very first glance one had of him. Whether you met him in the street or saw him in the Legislative Chamber, he was one of the first whose name you felt compelled to ask. He was an Irishman and a Roman Catholic, and bore an historic name. He was the Attorney-General for New South Wales. A peculiar-looking man, with a keen sense of duty and a strong, resolute will, John Hubert Plunkett left his mark in the history of his adopted country.

Dressed in black from head to foot, he sat in his office-chair, scanning with his dark eyes a thick pile of manuscript that lay on the table before him. In imagination one can picture his manner and mental absorption as his strong sense of justice was shocked and horrified by the terrible details which he read when they disclosed to him one of the most cruel tragedies that has stained the pages of our history with its crime. It was his business and inflexible duty as Grand Jury of the country to probe this matter to the very bottom, and to secure the awful punishment of the law for those who might be proved to be guily. As he read so, something like the following was made known to him :—

Away out in the far north-east parts of the colony, in

c

some of its most fertile and fair spots, the squatters were finding their way and occupying with their herds of cattle some of the richest pastoral lands, and were thus turning to account the wealth of grass and herbage that for untold ages had grown and passed away uncropped. It is a pleasant land to look upon, with its myall plains and alluvial valleys, and thinly - timbered, undulating downs and high blue mountain ranges bounding the horizon. It is a country of spring and summer seasons and where winter snows are never known. There was but one enemy of the white man there, if, indeed, he could be regarded as such, and that was the black aboriginal man—a creature not very hard to deal with, timid certainly, and probably at times somewhat treacherous, that is, when his rights—and he had rights—seemed to him to be unduly invaded. His treachery, such as it was, was the natural result of his weakness. Whatever his treachery might have been, this story tells us that he was far supassed in that unmanly vice by the white intruders into his country. It was not, at all events, charged against him as a ground of offence on this occasion. If for a moment we put ourselves into his place, we will see how irritating it must have been to him to be pushed away from the lands that his forefathers had roamed over from time immemorial—to be circumscribed in his liberty of hunting his natural and only supply of food in those places where he had preyed at will. Hunger, unfortunately, is one of those sensations that comes to a human being with irritating consciousness and a certain constant rapidity, and is no doubt very inconvenient; but somehow or another, it must be appeased. Each one, at least, thinks so of himself. Perhaps we are not quite so convinced of the necessity when we contemplate the desires of others, more especially when satisfying these desires interferes with us and our pleasures. Now, there is nothing that causes cattle to wander away from their homes more than men —and especially black men—walking about where they are depastured. So it came to pass that the blacks were not allowed to wander at pleasure, hunting kangaroo and emu, and chopping out the sleepy opossum everywhere as had been their custom. And as, without such hunting, they were not able to appease that tormenting thing called hunger, this hunger was proving rather a bar to the peaceful settlement of the country, and no doubt some illfeeling was thereby created between the two races.

The men who were employed as servants in carrying on this early pioneering business were "Government men," and although up to the time of the commencement of our story there is no evidence of any actual deadly conflict having taken place in these parts, still there had been some smouldering hostility; so much so, that the whites never went out on their business without carrying firearms with them. This more by way of defence than offence. However, now more peaceable relations seem to have been established, and at a squatter's station which a man named Kilminster had charge of this was especially evident. Up to this time Kilminster does not seem to have been a bad man. An energetic, faithful servant, and apparently a kindly man, he had made a truce with the black tribes of the place, had "made friends," as they said, and they were allowed to congregate at the station to the number of thirty or forty, and had the use of some of the huts. Kilminster's immediate superior, the overseer, had remonstrated with him for allowing the blacks to be about the place in such numbers, but at his earnest request they were permitted to take up their quarters there. And as he often danced and played with the "piccaninnies," and otherwise seemed to harbour no ill-

will, but rather the contrary, they appear to have enter-
tained no other than the friendliest feelings towards
him. Unfortunately, all this was to be changed on one
fateful Saturday evening. The previous Friday had
been very gloomy and wet, as though Nature herself
had some foreboding of an impending catastrophe.

Among this people, all unconscious of coming evil,
who were then in their camp, was Old Daddy, a tall,
erect old man, a very patriarch of the tribe, with a long
venerable grey beard, squatting under his sheet of bark,
with his opossum cloak thrown over his shoulders. As
he slowly smoked his pipe of tobacco (a new pleasure
learned from the whites) he warmed his hands over his
low fire, and now and again raked out a small live coal
ot revivify his pipe, and with eyes winking and blinking
as the breeze drove the smoke of his fire over him, he
looked a very picture of uncivilized barbarian contentment. Close to him, and circling round the fire, were
younger men, sitting tailor-like, one crooning in low,
monotonous, but not by any means harsh, tone, a tribal
hunting-song, all the while scratching with a sharp-
edged "bindoogan" shell the fleshy side of a dried
opossum's skin, doubled over on the thick muscles of
his naked thigh, and thus marking on the skin his
"totem." Another was shaping a boomerang from a
piece of wood cut from the bent elbow of a myall tree,
the heel of his left foot crossed over his right knee,
acting the part of the carpenter's bench, while he chop-
ped away at the wood with the point of a shear-blade,
a present from the whites, and of inestimable value.
Ippitha, a buxom young lubra, has just come to the camp
from the station-hut with the clothes of the white men to
wash, so that they may have them clean for the Sunday.
With large, dark, lustrous eyes, and white, even teeth,
and merry laugh and low, soft, musical voice, she has
learned to comb her hair in simple adornment and

behave with not unattractive feminine coquetry. Little
Charley (named after and by Kilminster, an intelligent
little fellow, three years old, learning to speak the whites'
language) utterly impotent and guileless, with others
like him, is rolling over and tumbling on the ground in
childish play and glee. They chase each other round
and through the camps, pretending to be enemies and
hunted animals, and now and again raise the ire of one
of the elders by their deafening shouts and laughter.
As he calls out at them they run away to a safe distance
and hurl back impudent defiance, and laugh again and
make their elders laugh at their very "cheekiness;" and
the camp is full of life and peaceful contentment.

But hark! the dull thud of unshod mounted horses
galloping along over the wet soft ground is heard.
Ippitha turns quickly round in the direction of the
coming sound, and the young men cease from their
work, and the old man listens, and the children become
silent, and run to the camps of their parents, and soon
a troop of horsemen—some ten or a dozen—are in sight.
As they come nearer, they pull up into a walking pace,
and the sun glints and flashes from guns and pistols
they are carrying. As the blacks watch the horsemen
approach, who encircle them, an instinctive feeling of
impending danger possesses them; and they start up
and run for the station-huts, the mothers snatching up
their children and carrying them in their arms. And
some eight and twenty of them crowd into the hut, for
their friend Charley Kilminster is there. And the men
(all stockmen from neighbouring stations) ride up, and
the blacks inside gather about the door and peer out at the
men with their great, dark, flashing eyes, like those of
some wild animals at bay in their den, and they talk
rapidly to each other in an undertone. And the horsemen dismount and talk with Kilminster, and he looks
white and anxious, and seems to be hovering between

duty and fear. His duty towards those who having sought it are under his protection—and his fear of his fellow white men. Alas! the duty gives way to the fear. And now one of the new-comers takes a long hempen rope from round his horse's neck and begins to unravel it, and he cuts the strands into convenient lengths, and one by one the unfortunate people who have trapped themselves are taken out of the trap and their hands are tied together. They are strung upon the remainder of rope like jet beads for a necklace.

In low plaintive tones they ask each other what it all means, and none can answer. And we may suppose them to appeal to Ippitha, who knows more of the white's ways, and whose relations with one of them has been of the tenderest character—they appeal to her in tremulous tones to learn, if possible, from her what it all means. Doubtless she tells them "she thinks it is all in fun. Is not Charley Kilminster there, who plays with and nurses their children on his knee, and who is their friend, and lets them stop at the place, and gives them bread and beef and tea? It is only stupid of them to think that Charley, her lover too, can do them any harm." And so the people are somewhat re-assured, and if it is to be only a joke they think they may tamely submit. Resistance now, at all events, seems to be impossible. And the poor creatures are led off, surrounded by their cruel captors. And now the joke becoming too serious, the women and the children (on their mothers' backs) begin to cry. One lubra, because she was thought to have "the gift of beauty," was alone left behind in the hut. The hutkeeper, one Anderson, as they were leaving, asked what they were going to do, "Oh," said they, "only going to take them away to the mountains to frighten them." He appeals to Kilminster, now armed with a sword, to let Ippitha and little Charley remain behind. He refused the request, and it is rumoured that his answer was " D—— them; no! Let the tail go with the hide." We can only hope that this, at least, is a fiction. Little Charley is not tied with the rest, but his father and mother (Sandy and Ippitha) are, so he trudges along stoutly after them. And so the procession goes out of sight, and Kilminster with them. One is tempted to ask, " What evil genius possessed this man that he should join in such a dreadful conspiracy? Was his previous friendship only a blind? Or had it been sincere?" We are inclined to the last supposition, and that he was weakly overcome by the others by whom the whole thing had been previously planned. This, too, was his excuse.

Some short time after, Anderson, who remained at the hut, and was in no way a party to the business, heard two shots fired, and after some hours the men came back themselves, and their two swords all bloodstained, and Kilminster carrying a sword all bloodstained; but the black people never came back—nor is little Charley ever seen alive again. The men all stay at the hut that night; and the next day, Sunday, the most of them ride away, but some stay with Kilminster, and they go out again the same way they went yesterday; and Anderson soon sees great columns of smoke rise in that direction.

And now Kilminster's superior, one Hobbs, who lived at another station some miles away, hears rumours of something dreadful having been done, and he comes to make inquiry. He is directed to the spot by the flights of eagles and hawks and other birds of prey, and on his way he sees the tracks of the men and of the blacks and the children, almost from the very hut door to the place of the massacre—thanks to the rains that fell on that Friday. Then he sees one of the frightfullest sights human being ever looked upon. There lay the remains of some twenty-eight human beings, all charred with fire and festering and torn, and partly devoured beyond all possibility of personal identification. The remains of men, women, and children lay there in a hideous, sickening, putrefying mass, and the bright Australian sun shining down upon it all.

The actual horrors of this terrible crime were never told: they can only be guessed at. The swords reeking with the blood of innocent children and helpless women. The piteous appeals for mercy in broken accents in a language little understood. The cruel awkwardness of men unskilled in the weapons they used. The gasping sighs; the protracted, lingering, agonizing deaths, that drew from the slayers brutal jokes and ribald jeers, are left altogether to the imagination to picture. It is well it is so. Let us hope the reality fell far short of the scene the mind will conjure up.

And to the overseer, then, Kilminster denies all complicity in the business; and the overseer, believing in his innocence, tells him he must write to his master. Then Kilminster implores him, "for the Lord Jesus Christ's sake" (the Lord Jesus being now too late remembered), not to send the letter, and the letter is torn up. Kilminster complains that the blacks frightened his cattle and caused them to wander; but the overseer rides out among the cattle and can find no evidence of such disturbance. And so this weak excuse was found to be untrue. And now the authorities hear of it, and a magistrate goes to the place to investigate the matter; and not without much trouble does he find any trace of the crime, for everything has been buried out of sight and smoothed over. And so it comes to be dealt with by the sallow, saturnine man sitting in his office chair, and he orders eleven men to be put upon their trial. And the day soon comes round when Mr. Justice William Burton, all clothed in scarlet and ermine, holds his court

in Sydney, and Kilminster and his companions are
placed in the dock, and are arrainged for the murder of
one Daddy, an aboriginal black of New South Wales,
and the whole is proved as told above, and further,
that the remains of one very tall black were found,
which were supposed to be those of Daddy. And the
Attorney-General conducts the prosecution, and he is
confronted by the three most eminent barristers of their
day—àBeckett and Windeyer and Foster,—and the
whole case is fully and fairly argued, and the judge sums
up, and the jury retire, and in a few minutes return with
a verdict of "Not Guilty." The indictment, it would
appear, was too particular. There was no absolute
proof that any of the remains were those of Daddy.
But the tall dark saturnine man, with the blood of the
innocent calling to him for vengeance, and with a stern
sense of righteous duty and virtuous indignation urging
him on, is not to be thus baulked of his rightful prey.
Another indictment at the same sitting of the court is
preferred against seven of these men, Kilminster being
one of them, and they are put again upon their trial for
the "murder of an aboriginal child, of a male and
female child, name unknown, and of Charley." The
whole of the evidence, word for word as before, is gone
through, and the same able and eloquent men skilled in
the law confront each other, and the judge sums up, and
the jury, better advised or more certain, find a verdict
of "Guilty," and the judge passes sentence, not without
much visible emotion ; and soon the last dread sentence
of the law is carried into effect. The seven men die on
the scaffold without making any sign of contrition or
confession, unless the fact that they asked permission of
the sheriff to shake hands with and kiss each other on
the gallows, which they did with streaming eyes, be
taken to be a sign of repentance.

And so at length Ippitha, with the large dark, lustrous eyes, and little Charlie, with the merry laugh and childish ways, and old Daddy, with the tall, erect figure and venerable snow-white beard, are avenged so far as their fellow-man is able to execute judgment. And the tall, sallow, saturnine man, with compassion in his heart for both the slayers and their victims, feels an inward satisfaction (even although it were done with extreme pain and mental agony) at having performed the high duty which he had been appointed to carry out "without fear, favour, or affection." Not fifty years have passed over since this was done, and the learned counsel and the Attorney-General, as well as the murderers and the slain, are all laid in the common dust.

It is not easy to account for the commission of this terrible and tragic baseness. These men were beyond police protection. It was thought by some who had better opportunity of judging, that it was done in consequence of a "scare," brought about by the fact of the large number of blacks congregating at this place. It was feared they intended mischief, and so the whites determined to be beforehand with them.

A PAIR OF OLD PISTOLS.

I AM sitting in that room of my house which, by a harmless euphemism, I call my "library." It is so dignified because there are a few bookshelves in it, with some volumes upon them. On the very topmost shelf there is a case containing a pair of duelling pistols of our grandfather's time. My home is built on the "ridge of a noble down." There are very extensive views from it over the country around the town of Bathurst. Between me and the town, as I now look through a window, there is a long gentle slope down to the wide rich holm that stretches away for a considerable distance on both sides of the sometime streamless and anon rushing flooded river. On a slightly elevated plateau on the opposite bank stands the town. As I see it through the thin mist of this cloudy August morning, its outlines are so softened as to give me the idea that the town and all it contains is but a vision or a dreamlike unreality. Were it not that my experience teaches me that the buildings and domes and spires I dimly see belong to veritable human houses, I feel sure that I should not feel much surprised if the whole were to dissolve with the renewal of sunshine, and leave no trace behind. So fairy-like and unsubstantial is the appearance through the veil which the exhalations from the earth moistened by the recent rains have drawn between me and it.

This indefinitiveness suits my train of thought, which is carrying me back through the shadowy past where the actors glide with ghostly silence and spiritual mystery. My view to the westward is down the valley with its broad alluvial fields, now brilliantly green in the coming spring. The serpentine course of the river as it meanders through the rich lands is marked here and there by solitary trees, and further on by a dense fringe of native oaks. Their dark branches are relieved in contrast by the light-green weeping willows which grow beside them under the river banks. These are just now bursting into leaf, and are like domes of green gossamer, so airy and delicate are they in their earliest frondescence. Undulating uplands everywhere stretch away from the river flats, and are naturally destitute of trees. They extend for miles, and are backed by the primeval forests. They are now under cultivation, and are dotted over by mansions and farmers' cottages, and are subdivided into numberless enclosures, and are as green as the proverbial wheat fields, which in reality they are. The forest encroaches here and there in long promontories upon the open downs, the dark olive and grey tints of the trees contrasting strongly with the green fields. Away to the far west and south and east, my view is across the gentle undulations, all cropped and green, to the lofty distant blue ranges, rising some 2000 feet above me. The prospect has the appearance of a large beryl set round with massive amethysts. As the season advances, the warmer rays of the sun will, with wonderful alchemy, transmute the blue-green beryl through chrysoprase into golden topaz as the wheat fields ripen and furnish their grain with all its life-bearing possibilities. There is no inanimate object so worthy of reverence as a wheat field ripening for the reaper. In its presence I always feel an inclination to uncover my head and make obeisance to its all-sustaining power. Hamlet finds a morbid, melancholy, philosophic pleasure in tracing the dust of Cæsar till it serves some ignoble use. May we not reverse the process and conceive of the highest intellectual achievements and material activities of mankind as lying latent in the potentialities of a wheat field. As I look from my window and see the evidences of weathering upon the surface upon the country, and the undoubted remains of vast volcanic action, my fancy will take me through "the infinite azure of the past," and ponder at the untiring energies of nature in for ever moulding and varying the beautiful outlines. In such contemplation one is reminded of the old fairy tale of the "Sleeping Princess," who, having grown in ever-increasing beauty through the countless ages, is awaiting the kiss of the prince (man's labour and toil) to wake her into active life and productive usefulness.

Just under my house is a little valley that comes through the forest and then on into the open plain. In it, at the very edge of the timbered land, there stands a clump of very large old manna-bearing gums. They are especially interesting to me, because I am told that under their shade in the early colonial days two men faced each other with deadly weapons in their hands. One at least sought the life of the other. That other— whose name I bear—with a—was it a perverted?—sense of honour, became a party to the business, because the sentiment of the time led him to feel that disgrace would attach to him if he refused. "Verdammt, the little spitfire!" as Teufelsdrockh has it, "God must needs laugh outright, could such a thing be, to see his wondrous mannikins here below." In those days a man had to do it or else be branded as a coward and for ever forfeit the esteem of his fellow spitfires, if not of the supposed amused Divinity, the opinion of the Divinity in such cases being little heeded. More than fifty years ago a gentleman, who had been a West Indian planter, made his home on the Bathurst Plains, having a right to a land grant, and, what is of more importance to our story, bringing with him a beautiful girl, his daughter. Marriageable young ladies of such a high class were not very common here in those days.   One of the neighbors, a young grazier, was an industrious native-born Australian, standing six feet in his stockings.   As he had cut his teeth on a corncob, he had all the strength and energy that that early and nutritious diet gave.   He was remarkable for his sterling character and good-natured disposition.   He was just then of a very susceptible age, and was wanting a wife for his prospering home.   The young people met, were pleased with each other, and a tender understanding seems to have been agreed upon between them.   The father neither gives nor withholds his consent; so the lovers patiently wait till his caution shall have exhausted itself.   But now a disturbing element appears upon the scene in the person of a young Scotchman.   He has brought some money out with him, wants a wife, and is inclined to make up to the young lady.   The father, after taking counsel with a friend, favours the pretensions of the new-comer.   The rivals scowl at each other, and as such a condition of things is not conducive to the orderly well-being and peace of the household, the young Australian is forbidden the premises.   With the lady on his side, he is not to be so easily put off, and clandestine meetings are held at the " willow pond," under the shade of some great trees which grow there, and are dimly seen in the distance from my window.   All this (to them) intolerable interference excites the ire of the father and the accepted lover, and it ends in the rival being challenged to fight a duel with mortal weapons.

The father, by pre-arrangement with the now accepted lover, strange to say, is to be the principal in the affair. The discarded lover, under the rigid code of honour then in force and not being wanting in physical courage, accepts the challenge.   The lethal instruments to be used are on the table before me. They were made by one John Prosser, gunmaker, No. 9, Charing Cross, London. Mr. Prosser does not appear to have been at all ashamed of his share in the possibility of such transactions. He has deeply inlaid on the barrels a small piece of gold with his name graven on it, to be had in remembrance. They are an old pair of pistols with flint locks and hair triggers and heavy silvered butts. The original owner of them who brought them to the colony was an officer — Captain John Piper — in the 102nd regiment—the New South Wales Corps. As he was one of the seconds in the first civilized duel ever fought on Australian soil, that between Colonel Paterson and Captain Macarthur on September 14, 1801, these pistols were most probably used then. They were borrowed by the seconds for the occasion we are writing of. The party met under the large trees in the little valley, and the distance was measured off, and the principals stood ready for the word of command. When that was given, one report only was heard: the father did his best to shoot his adversary, as the bullet grazing his cheek fully testified.

The other, who under no provocation whatever could be induced to harm the father of her he loved so much, slowly and deliberately turns aside and discharges his pistol, directing it with harmless intention high up into the air. The father, with murder in his heart, now knowing that he will not be fired at, expresses himself as not satisfied, and demands another trial. So much courage and generosity is at least remarkable. The seconds, however, will not consent, aud so the affair ends, and the accepted Scotchman lover marries the somewhat unwilling lady. And in two years' time she is laid in her grave. And the husband, having lost his wife, sails away to other lands, but neither he nor the ship is ever seen or heard of again after they leave this shore. The Australian marries also and becomes very prosperous, and has numerous offspring. He, when the time comes, is entrusted by his fellow-colonists with a representative office of responsibility and trust—a position he holds for nearly a third of a century. He lived beyond the allotted time of man's life and died crowned with the respect and love of all who knew him, and over forty years after was put to rest near the same spot with her for whose sake he had risked his life.

Whenever I am tempted to act meanly or despicably I contemplate these old pistols, and find a wholesome mental tonic in bringing to my recollection the part my progenitor played in this little drama—wondering, too, how much this early, sorrowful experience, and the standing so close to the verge of a great sin, had in moulding his character to that loving gentleness and tolerance which he always showed to all with whom he came in contact. For it is sometimes good for a man that his soul should be darkened by the shadow of possible, if not actual, guilt. To the wise man such a condition brings with it repentant humility and world-wide toleration, and sympathetic softness towards his erring fellow-creatures.

And now the mists have cleared away, and the sunshine reveals all; and the distant town, with its ruddy walls in rich warm colouring, glows as cornelian amid the fields of emerald hue, and stands out in strong relief against the opaline lustre or the sky. But the present only is bright. The past is softened and obscured, and is haunted by ghostly silences and melancholy memories.

THE HUNDREDWEIGHT OF GOLD.

OME time in the "thirties" of the present century, a young Irish doctor came out to New South Wales in charge of a human freight, with hopes of better fortune. Warm-hearted and full of genial humour, his laugh was one of the most contagious pieces of merriment ever human being was blessed with. His wildest dreams when he landed here never promised such a romantic accident as this story tells actually befel him. He settled at Bathurst, married, tried his profession, combined farming with pharmacy, and finding the air here too salubrious for profitable employment of the latter, and markets too limited to make the former pay, took to wool growing. He had notions somewhat Quixotic, perhaps, as to what was derogatory to his profession, and declined to send out any bills for overdue fees. He used to boast that he was the first to grow wheat on the high lands of Bathurst Plains. If that were so—and I have no reason to doubt it—he must be awarded credit as being a pioneer of the agricultural prosperity of the district, The early settlers here, like the farmers of the Hawkesbury, cultivated only the alluvial flats of the river. Dr. William John Kerr secured a small sheep station called Wallerwaugh, situated on the high land lying between the Macquarie River and the Meroo Creek, and there lived in quiet retirement, tending his small flock, and occasionally practising his profession as a labour of love. It was a region where no medical man, as such, could be induced to go for money, if indeed money was to be found there at all. So the doctor, as his neighbours fell ill, simply practised for love, and earned and won a good deal of it. I have known him ride forty miles to relieve a sick child, and no one ever thought of offending him by offer of fee. On these charitable journeys he was often accompanied by his wife—one of the gentlest, kindest, and most lovable and unselfish of human creatures—whose delight was in cheerful, modest self-sacrifice when the good of others demanded it. She was often the voluntary nurse of her husband's free patients. This pair lived in a neat little cottage in a secluded valley among the hills of that remote part. Their neighbours for miles round were isolated shepherds and their families, and these were few and far between. With the conservatism that comes with increasing years, and contrasting the present with the past times, I look back with a feeling of pleasant, wishful regret at the state of society then existing. We were a simple-minded people in those days, and knew little or nothing of that feverish anxiety, that hurry and worry and scramble for wealth that came in when "the gold broke out." We were given to much neighbourliness, and to kind and simple and unostentatious hospitality. Everybody knew everybody, and everybody was always a welcome guest. The employers as a rule were their servants' best friends. I knew many servants whose lifelong fidelity would have spared no pains in the care of their master's property. But alas! we have changed all that. Among the doctor's dependents was a small tribe of aboriginal blacks, who had charge of two flocks of sheep. The names of three connected with our story were Jemmy Irving, Long Tommy, and Tommy Bumbo. Of these, the first two had received some little instruction in the old mission school at Wellington when under the charge of the late Revs. Canon

Günther and W. Watson. These three were very different in character. Jemmy was calm, sedate, and even a little bit dignified; Long Tommy was rather a sour, surly customer, of great stature and strength; Tommy Bumbo, although claiming to be the son of a king, was an amusing little larrikin, up to all sorts of fun and mischief, I think they were all civilised into a taste for " grog and tobacco." When gold was first discovered in the colony in May, 1851, the news reached the ears of these blacks, and stimulated them to hunt for it. Jemmy had known of the discovery of gold by McGregor near Wellington some years before, and he meant to keep his keen eyes open. One day in the month of June, 1851, while following the tail of his flock over a low ridge, on the crest of which there stood np some feet above the surface a broad, well-defined reef of quartz, Jemmy saw three pieces of detached rock. With a black's curiosity, he tried to turn over the larger with his stick. It proved to be so much heavier than his previous experience of quartz stones of that size expected that he determined to unravel the mystery. As he stooped down, he then noticed, lying beside this stone, and quite exposed, a piece of yellow metal. Jemmy thought it looked something like the stuff he had seen once or twice in his life in the shape of a sovereign. He then turned over the stone, and behold the whole of the under surface was a mass of the same material. As seventy pounds of gold were afterwards knocked out of it, no wonder Jemmy found it heavier than ordinary quartz. " I believe this one gold : mine yan 'long master now, and tell it that one," was his first thought. But before heading his sheep for home, he examined the two smaller rocks, and they too were very heavy, and highly charged with the same mysterious yellow stuff. As he ponders over the discovery, his quick ear detects an approaching footstep. A white man, a shepherd of a neighbouring sheep farmer, by accident feeding his flock near the place that day, is coming to have a smoke and a "yarn" with him, As the shepherd approaches Jemmy drops his blanket over the stones and sits upon it. They fill their pipes and smoke and talk for an hour or more, but Jemmy neither budges nor says a word about the gold, although, the chief discourse is about the metal and how to find it. When the white man goes he tells Jemmy he means to give up his charge and turn digger and advises him to do the same. His subsequent disappointment may be imagined.

The next morning Jemmy went to the head station. In my mind's eye I can see the doctor, as was his wont, enjoying his after-breakfast pipe in deep reverie, marching with slippered feet up and down the verandah of his cottage, while Jemmy is coming to tell him the wonderful story, I can hear the doctor's incredulous laugh and exclamation "Fudge!" until the blackfellow produces the small nugget of about 2oz. weight which he found near the large one. Then the doctor thinks there may be something in it, although this piece looked more like tarnished brass than bright gold. However, the place was only a few miles distant, so the horses were saddled, and the doctor and his wife, with Jemmy trotting along on foot beside them, started off. A very lonely spot it was there in the heart of the primeval forest of great white gums and stringy barks. The rocks were examined, and then incredulity vanished, and more than the hopes of years—the fact of a fortune secured in a moment, and without thought and labour—forced itself upon the bewildered mind of the doctor. The position realized, an empty flour-bag, in which to place the treasure, was procured from the blacks' camp, and the great mistake was made of breaking up the stones. The owner always regretted having done this. With these wonderful rocks, containing at that time the largest mass of native gold ever known to have been discovered, what an opening for more fortune to travel through the world and exhibit them! This was the thought when too late, after a few blows from Jemmy's tomahawk had broken them into a thousand fragments. The pieces were carefully gathered up and taken home. The first act then of the doctor, in the exuberance of his generosity, was to present his faithful shepherds with the two flocks of sheep and the right to so much of his run as would keep them. When the rush of diggers set in to this spot shortly after, the blacks and their sheep became the objects of particular attention to some not very scrupulous gentlemen. Most of the sheep were parted with for grog and tobacco, and the remnant were bought for a song by a neighbouring sheep-owner, who, seeing a chance for a bargain made it there and then. While his friends admired the conscientous act of the doctor in so liberally rewarding his faithful shepherds, they could not refrain from accusing him of folly, considering his generosity had much better have found vent in a less liberal but more useful way. However, it little matters now, as all the parties have long since gone to their rest.

Then came the question, What shall we do with it? Secrecy was enjoined upon the blacks, and the doctor and his wife, with the treasure in a pair of leather saddle bags, started for Bathurst, some sixty miles distant. The first night was passed at a head sheep station of my father's at Pyramul. A man attended to see after the horses, but the doctor contrived that no one should touch the bags but himself. "Yer bags seem mighty heavy," said John O'Brien, the man aforesaid, as the doctor tried, with careless unconcern to throw them across the paling fence; "is it goold ye have in them?" "Faith it is," said the doctor; "what else would I be carrying in these times?" This open confession had the desired effect, for John, with a loud laugh at its obvious absurdity, did not believe a word of it. John afterwards took great credit to himself for his acute sagacity. The next day they passed the Turon River, where gold had lately been discovered by Mr. Owen Murnane, my father's overseer at Pyramul. This field was just then being rushed by gold-seekers from all parts of the colonies. Such a "motley crew" surely was never before seen on this world gathered together for a common purpose. All sorts and conditions of men were there—lawyers, doctors, merchants, bankers, squatters, clerks from city offices, shepherds, stockmen, prizefighters, men representing every trade and profession under the sun, all turned diggers. The good-humoured orderliness of the crowd was surprising. I remember well the appearance of the Turon before this influx. A lonely valley between high and rocky precipitous mountain ranges, and in which a stream of beautifully clear water rippled melodiously over a very stony bed, filling very large holes, which literally swarmed with cod and other fish. The whole river bed was shaded by a dense grove of dark and melancholy sighing native oaks. A valley rarely, if ever, visited by any but some solitary shepherd and stray stockman, was now suddenly alive with crowds of human beings, its rocks echoing to songs and shouts and laughter, and all the sounds of a great busy multitude; its banks at night lit up by a thousand camp fires. Verily a most pleasant and romantic place to hold such a monstrous picnic, and revel in dreams of rapid fortune. The doctor and his mysterious load passed unheeded by, unless the humourous crowd "baa'd" him as he went. This was the customary salute to all new comers, who were at once recognised as such, and continued in force for a year or more in the early digging days. The practice was commenced at Ophir, in order to bewilder an old shepherd, who, while watching the diggers there, frequently lost his sheep, and then old Jack was deceived by plaintive bleats on all sides. It was extended next to all diggers seen carrying pieces of mutton from the extempore butcher's shops, and at last all new comers were so treated, the whole multitude joining in the sheepish chorus until they became tired, or the object of this ridiculous greeting passed out of sight. I remember a stalwart digger silencing this kind of welcome. He was carrying half a sheep over his shoulder, when he was seen, and the usual baa-ing commenced. "Ah," shouted he, "it is easy knowing where his head is." With his easily gotten treasure, how the doctor must have laughed in his sleeve at all these anxious gold-seekers, most of whom were turning over tons of earth for a few grains. My father's house at Brucedale was reached that evening. The bags were carried inside and deposited in a secret place with more ceremony than their outward appearance seemed to justify. The doctor and myself strolled out to the stables. I noticed that he seemed anxious and preoccupied. I think, even then, he was not quite sure that the treasure would not turn out to be a delusive fairy gift and fade away. The metal might not be gold after all. My father joined us. "What, in the name of fortune, have you got in the bags, doctor?" (The doctor's wife, my father's sister, it appears, had breathed a suspicion.) "Is it gold?" "I believe it is," said he. "Nonsense," said my father. "Here is a piece of it," said the doctor, taking out of his pocket the two-ounce nugget. After examining it, "By Jove, I believe it is," was the answer. The doctor gave me that two-ounce piece, and by its means I made the acquaintance of Chaucer, and Spencer and Shelley, Coleridge and Tennyson, very dear friends, who have been most reverenced and beloved lodgers with me ever since. Some of the household were let into the secret, and silence commanded. That night, after a few chance guests who were in the house, had retired, the bags were brought out, and their con-tents displayed to our wondering, delighted, and eager gaze. Two large pieces, weighing nearly seven pounds each, were much admired. The owner had named these the Queen and Prince Albert nuggets. Not an hour must be lost. As soon as arrangements could be made, a party was formed, and, headed by the doctor, proceeded to the spot. Some seven of us started. Gold, of course, was to be had there by the ton weight. We were all to be millionaires. Crœsus was very " small potatoes " as a man of wealth compared with our ex-pectations. The desirability of taking out a bullock dray to bring back our treasure, was, if not very seri-ously, discussed, at least not thought to be too supremely absurd. In view of the quantities we were to get, as much as for their own convenience, my father drove the doctor in a dog-cart and tandem. It was well to be provided for a contingency. Our party aroused no sus-picion. My father's sheep stations lay out in that direction. His journey in that way was then quite natural. We did not even whisper to ourselves of our great expectations for fear foreign ears should hear. Two days, and we reached the spot. For two or three more we searched diligently, aided by the blacks, who unearthed a nugget of nine ounces weight, part of which protruded above the surface. We knocked off specks of gold from the great reef, and, at length thoroughly disappointed, we determined, somewhat sadly, to return home. We reached the Turon at mid-day on Sunday. Having no further reason for concealment, the story was told. The news soon spread. " Up and away " was the order of the day, as a regular stampede of dig-gers took place—most of them travelling all that night in order to arrive first at the spot. Next day, Monday, much to the relief of the ladies, who were left at home

in sole possession, my father with the doctor, my brother Frank, and myself, took the gold to Bathurst for
the purpose of depositing it in the Union Bank.   As we
drove slowly up the last steep pinch of the Pine Hills,
a body of men, mostly armed, met us.   We at first
thought it was a case of "stick up." They were honest;
having heard of the find, they were off to join the rush.
We showed them the gold, gave them information as
to the locality; they thanked us, gave us three cheers,
and went hopefully on their way.   The visibility and
tangibility of so much wealth so easily obtained was
almost enough to raise hope in a dead man.   As
the town was near, the two large pieces were given
to my brother and self to hold.   We passed a man: we
held them out to him at arm's length.   He stopped,
stared, grinned, and set off after us full speed.

The news that we were coming reached Bathurst the
night before, so that everyone was on the look-out for
our appearance.   In a few seconds the whole town was
at our heels.   We drew up opposite the newspaper
office, then in William-street, where Kite's buildings
now are.   The crowd surrounded us.   Such excitement!
Such insane delight!   Everyone wants to see, touch,
and handle.   The two large nuggets are unreservedly
passed to the people.   They are lost sight of!   Who's
got them now?   There is a surge of the crowd to the
other side of the street as our old friend and
long-time citizen, Mr. Josiah Parker, with a nugget
under each arm, runs off with them to his shop
to weigh them.   Everybody's curiosity gratified, we
recover our treasure, and are allowed to go to the
bank, where the mass was weighed, and turned the
scale at over 104℔.   The actual weight—the doctor
having given away over 2℔. of crumbs—was more
than 106℔. of sold gold.

The news of the great find soon reached Sydney, and

a memher of the firm of Thacker, Daniel and Co. came up to effect a purchase. The lot was sold at £3 7s. 6d. per oz. The Government wrote to Mr. Commissioner Hardy to the effect that they had heard rumours of an extraordinary nature, expressed surprise that he had made no report, and wanted to know what steps he had taken. The Commissioner misconstrued this into an order to seize the gold, which he did. The Government did not intend this, but having got possession, they were loath to part with it. The country cried "Shame!" and, after some little delay, the gold was given up on conditions, and in due time found its way into the great melting pot of the English mint. A piece of the gold was saved by my aunt (Mrs. Kerr) and given to her father. It is now mine, and weighs about 5½oz., and is a remarkably beautiful specimen of "gold in the quartz," the metal being of bright yellow colour, prettily frosted, and the quartz of a pink tinge.

As soon as the news reached England, the "gold fever" broke out there, and a perfect mania for promoting companies to work the fields here seized hold of the people. Some companies were formed, and the officers of two of them at least reached Bathurst, and one of them actually carried on operations in the reef where the hundredweight was found. My father's name having found its way into the prints, both here and in England in connection with this find, a solicitor in London wrote to him offering him £10,000 (ten thousand pounds) for his name and a piece of land, to be used in floating a company in London. It was explained that it was not necessary that gold should have been found upon the land. The case would be fully met if the land was somewhere in the district of the great find. I shall not easily forget the indignation with which my father refused the tempting offer. "The d—— ——!" said he. Now my father never cursed anyone unless the circumstances of the case fully and justly demanded such an expression of righteous anger. My respect for him was much increased, if that were possible, by this outbreak and justifiable commination. "The d—— scoundrel, he wants to make me his tool to swindle the British public!" As I said before, we were a simple-minded people in those days, and were very innocent of promoting our own grasping propensities at the expense of the general public. This solicitor was wanting in professional courtesy, for, strange to say, he never acknowledged the receipt of my father's answer. He felt some delicacy in again trusting his London polish to be ruthlessly tarnished by such an uncivilized colonial. Measured by the conscience of a later day in these matters—he had auriferous land in the neighbourhood—my father may be judged to have acted unwisely. My impression is that the refusal of that offer was not the least part of his children's inheritance.

The finding of this mass of gold had a very great effect in turning the eyes of the world to these colonies. Within a yard or two of the same spot, a few inches under the surface, a nugget of 28℔. weight was soon after found. Large quantities were got in the alluvial bed of the Louisa (corrupted from the native name, "Ill-ou-e-jah,") Creek, which seldom ran, close by. I am not aware that much was found in the reef, although a great deal of capital was expended upon it. The main incidents of the story are used by Charles Reade in his great novel, "Never Too Late to Mend."

WESTERN REBELLIONS.

BLACK AND WHITE.

IF one travels some sixteen miles to the north-west from the city of Bathurst, he will, after passing over some steep granite-crowned ranges of hills, drop in long descent into a series of small, pretty valleys. Embosomed in the hills and encircled by high, rocky ranges, the place is secluded and very romantic-looking. On a sloping knoll stands an old stone-walled cottage. At the time of the commencement of our story in 1824 a considerable area of the land about these valleys had been granted to an emigrant gentleman from the old land. Peaceful and quiet as the spot is at the time of our present writing, it has been the scene of a dastardly massacre. In the year above mentioned, a foreigner named Antonio had cultivated a patch of land on the Macquarie River, opposite the town of Bathurst. Among other things he grew some potatoes. One day, as a large number of the black tribe of the place came by, Antonio, moved by a spirit of good nature, gave some of his tubers to these people. Next day, they having appreciated the gift, appeared at the potato patch and commenced to help themselves. This was not to Antonio's liking, who roused the people of the settlement in his behalf. They rushed down and attacked the blacks, some of whom were killed and others maimed. After this, the blacks commenced general depredations, killing solitary shepherds, destroy-

ing large numbers of sheep, and they actually got possession of seven stand of arms and some ammunition. In
the course of a short time, hostile contests having taken
place, several aborigines, as well as Europeans, were
killed. To put a stop to these proceedings, martial law
was proclaimed through all the country lying west of
Mount York. Under this condition of things the
blacks were shot down without any respect. Getting
the worst of it, most of them made out into the deep
dells of the Capertee country, and, although some
escaped, many were killed there. At the place we are
writing of a camp of blacks had been established. The
proclamation of martial law was as undecipherable to
them as an Egyptian hieroglyph. This mattered little
to the whites—the fiat had gone forth and must be acted
upon. So a party of soldiers was despatched to deal
with those at this camp. Negotiations, apparently
friendly, but really treacherous, were entered into.
Food was prepared, and was placed on the ground
within musket range of the station buildings. The
blacks were invited to come for it. Unsuspectingly they
did come, principally women and children. As they
gathered up the white men's presents they were shot
down by a brutal volley, without regard to age or sex.
The great black leader of the day, named Windradyne,
alias Saturday, was so offensive that 500 acres of land
were offered for his capture. Saturday lived through
this martial law business, and was afterwards killed by
one of his own countrymen in a duel. He is said to
have been really a fine specimen of the manly savage.
For some time before his death he lived in peace with
the whites, and stories are told of his goodnatured and
affectionate conduct towards the children of his former
foes. When martial law had run its course, extermination is the word that most aptly describes the result. As
the old Romans said, " They made a solitude and

called it peace." The last effort of a doomed race was thus ended.

The white rebellion took place in 1830. At a station near the one above mentioned, the shearing of 1829 was being performed as usual in the spring months. The methods were primitive, although the shearing was better done then than now. "Tomahawking" and "hundred a day men" were altogether unknown. The wool was cut off closely and evenly, and the staple maintained in full length throughout. The wasteful second cut of the present day, as your "flash ringer" chops out through the fleece over the backbone of the sheep, and then taking a second "blow," cutting your fleece and the staple in two, making good "combing" into short "clothing," was never allowed. Most of the shearers of that day could shear in the old-fashioned English manner, and show the "rib and quarter" in proper style. A fat sheep so shorn is really a pretty work of art. Alas for the past! The shed under which the shearing was done was a very simple structure of slab and bark; not one of our modern shepherd kings' palaces, costing thousands. The wool was put into the bales by the aid of a spade. At the back of the shed was a bullock-dray being loaded with the bales of wool as they were pressed. The bullock-driver, one Robert Entwistle, is a fine, stalwart young Englishman, the early prototype, possibly, of Henry Kendall's delightful "Bullocky Bill."

> .   .   .   "In the circles select
> Of scholars he hasn't a place ;
> But he walks like a man with his forehead erect,
> And he looks at God's day in the face."

He has probably been exiled to Australia for some youthful folly. No doubt he was known as "Bob," with a qualifying adjective descriptive of some personal peculiarity. He was a good servant, and was wholly trusted by his master. His ticket-of-leave was due, on receipt of which he could work for wages as a free man. No black mark so far stood against him in the record. His ambition was, by honest industry, to wipe out the stain on his character, to obtain a piece of land, to marry a wife, and become altogether a good and reputable colonist. As his ticket was due, he need not have worked any longer for his master. This gentleman, however, had been kind and considerate to him, and Bob, not being ungrateful, agreed to take the load of wool to Sydney and return with the station supplies. When as much as the dray will carry was put upon it, Bob and his "off-side driver" yoked up the team to start on their long journey. Before their bullocks were straightened out for their task, the master appeared with a bottle and a tumber and they drank his health in a stiff glass of rum, and the master wishes them a "pleasant trip." This ceremony over, Bob picks up his long whip and, whirling it round his head, touches up the rump of the off-side leader pretty sharply with the silken lash. The team wriggle like a snake, and as the leaders bend to the yoke they then straighten out, and the dray, with heavy dull rattle, moves on, and groans and creaks under its weighty load. In due time, in company with a neighbour's dray similarly loaded, Bob arrives at Bathurst and camps for dinner on the bank of the Macquarie River some mile or so from the "settlement," as the small village surrounding the Government buildings was then called.

The appearance of the river was very different then from the ugly chasm or monstrous ditch which we now behold. Perhaps it has altered itself in spite at being called by the harsh name of Macquarie; the native name "Wambool," meaning "meandering," being much more euphonious and appropriate. If the river has any feeling at all one can understand its restiveness under its new nomenclature.   The sun was hot and the roads were dusty, and as Bob and his mates scrambled down the grassy bank to the reed-fringed pond and stood on a small shelf formed by the roots of a large river oak tree, which overshadowed the deep pool of clear water, and filled their quart pots, the idea occurred to them that it would be very pleasant to have a bathe. The water was deep, and just such a place as heathen divinities might have chosen to disport themselves in. They strip off their clothes and plunge in, and dive to the depths and swim about—splashing the water over each other with much shouting and laughter, under the exhilarating influence of the cool and cleansing fluid. As they are thus enjoying themselves, suddenly—some hundred yards away, at the ford—a large cavalcade, following a vehicle containing an officer in uniform, dashes into the stream.   Governor Darling has arrived, and has been met and is being escorted to the " Settle-ment " by all who were the lucky possessors of horses. As they swarm into the river, most of them allow their animals to drink at the stream.   In a few minutes they disappear up the bank, following after his Excellency. Our bathers were astounded at this apparition, of the coming of which they knew nothing.   At the first appearance, however, instinctively they allowed them-selves, all but their heads, to be covered under the water. Unfortunately for them, Mr. E———, the Police Magis-trate of the district in attendance upon the Governor, had seen them.   He was a martinet of extravagant refinement, and was, or thought he ought to have been, shocked at what he had seen.   As the men are quietly eating their dinner some constables come to them with orders to arrest them and take them before his Worship. They submit, although they are all unwitting of having wilfully committed any offence.   The magistrate has them brought before him.   No excuse will avail them.

" Had he not seen them with his own eyes ? Perhaps "
—more horrible idea—" the Governor had even seen
them." Justice can only be done by sentencing such
villains to be flogged, and in Bob's case of cancelling
his "ticket-of-leave." Their backs are bared for the
" cat," and Bob's skin, which has hitherto been scarless,
and was as white and healthy as a maiden's breast, is
shortly covered with great bruised wales and blood-
streaked markings. He shuts his teeth and clenches
his hands and makes no murmur as he nerves himself
for the punishment. When his shirt is put on him
after he is cast loose, Robert Entwistle is an altered
man. He glares at his tormentors like some wild
animal. A sense of the gross injustice of his treatment almost maddens him. His heart, so lately so
full of the hope of a prosperous and not unhonored
future, is now boiling with hatred and revenge. He goes
on his way an altered man. Not till some ten months
after this scene has he matured his scheme, all this
time nursing his wrath and his revenge. He is a mas-
terful man in his way, and has by this time induced a
number of his fellows to rob their employers of arms
and ammunition and join him in the bush. They, to
the number of about twenty, go from station to station
compelling others to go with them. In a large party
they proceed to the pastoral farm of the police magistrate, near the now little railway station of Wimbledon.
The magistrate is not there: his overseer is in charge
of the place. Had the master been there, no doubt a
short reckoning would have been made. Our sympathy
with Entwistle must now end, for, on the overseer
refusing to join them, they threaten to shoot him. He
tells them " they are not game." A foolish challenge to
an exasperated man, for Entwistle then shoots him in
the breast. Not being killed at once, another of the
gang shoots at him; the poor man then falls on the floor

of the hut, and crawls to the fireside, and then dies. A deed so cruel and unprovoked and useless leaves the perpetrators outside our sympathy.

As soon as the news of this outrage reaches the settlement, Major Macpherson, the officer in charge of the small detachment of soldiers stationed there, convenes a meeting of the inhabitants. Twelve gentlemen volunteer to form a small cavalry force and follow the murderers. That evening, just as they are about to start, news arrives that the bushrangers have robbed Mr. Arkell's station at Campbell's River. The little force at once push on for that place, where they arrive at daylight. Their chosen leader, the late W. H. Suttor, with his brother Charles (now an octogenarian, who has a lively recollection of the business) as second in command, secure the services of two blacks. All the next day the blacks track the gang, and about an hour before sunset they come in sight of the camp on a low-lying clear hill, situated between Trunkey and the Abercrombie River, and known as "Bushrangers' Bald Hill" to the present day. The second in command takes a part of the force with him in order to secure a position to cut off the retreat of the enemy. Unfortunately, one of the volunteers, either misjudging the distance or through nervousness, fired a futile shot at the camp, with no other effect than that of alarming the occupants, who at once took up positions behind trees, and commenced to fire at the advancing party. These also disposed of themselves in the same manner, and a sharp contest took place. Entwistle, with his hat covered with a profusion of ribbons, urged on his men, and directed them to make sure of the leader, whom he supposed to be his foe, the police magistrate. So these two parties of men blaze away at each other somewhat harmlessly. It was estimated that some 300 rounds must have been discharged. Two of the hushrangers were wounded, but were not killed. The leader of the attacking party had a bullet through his hat, and eighteen bullets were found to have hit the small tree behind which he stood. Ammunition now failing the volunteers, they made a charge, intended as a feint, upon which the gang took to flight. As night was coming on, it was impossible to follow them further with any chance of success, so the volunteers fell back upon Arkell's out-station. A servant of Arkell's was ordered to watch the horses all night, but either from neglect of duty—the rain poured in torrents the while—or from sympathy with the marauders, he allowed the horses to escape. The next day, a party of police under Lieutenant Brown came up and followed the retreating gang. They saw them making off over a high range ; they pushed on after them. On reaching the summit of the range they were met with a volley from the pursued, who had ensconced themselves behind trees and rocks. Two of the police and five of their horses were killed. Discomfited, the force were obliged to retire. The next thing heard of these desperate men was at the Lachlan River (native name " Cullahree"), where they committted depredations at Ranken's Station. Here they were met by Lieutenant Macalister with police from Goulburn. An encounter took place, when Macalister and several men on both sides were wounded. A drawn battle declared apparently. However, on the next day Captain Walpole, with a detachment of soldiers, who had marched from Sydney at the first news of the outbreak, now joined the police under Macalister. All things considered, this march of Walpole's was a wonderful business. The bushrangers, seeing such a strong force, considered their case hopeless, and surrendered. A special Assize Court was held at Bathurst, when the men, to the number of ten, were tried and convicted of the murder of the overseer. They went to their death

in what is called a hardened manner, praying that the
sentence be speedily carried out, so that they might
be at once put out of their misery; which statement makes one ponder not a little.

And so some thirteen lives were lost, and many others
jeopardised, because a bullock-driver cleansed himself
in the Macquarie River. If the Governor had only been
half-an-hour earlier or later; if Entwistle had declined
to oblige his master; if the magistrate had had some
more bowels of compassion and less niceness. But what
is the use of "iffing?" The thing was done, and as
long as the universe stands it can never be undone,
although we may find 10,000 ifs and reasons why it
had been better left undone.

The story of these two rebellions goes to show
what is so often insisted upon, that most disastrous
results may spring from very small causes; or, in other
words, "how great a matter a little fire kindleth."

The graves of these men were to be seen in the old
burial ground in George-street, Bathurst. Five were
laid in each grave.

THE VAN DIEMEN'S LAND GHOULS.

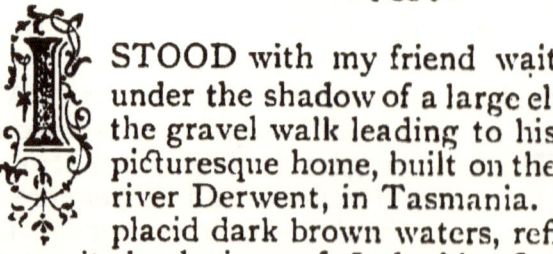

STOOD with my friend waiting for the coach
under the shadow of a large elm tree that shades
the gravel walk leading to his oldfashioned and
picturesque home, built on the steep bank of the
river Derwent, in Tasmania. The river, with its
placid dark brown waters, reflecting everything
upon its banks in perfect double, flowed with scarcely
perceptible advance just beneath us. I have never seen

such illusive natural reflections anywhere as are to be seen in this stream. I have photographs of scenery on its banks, and it is difficult to decide at first glance which is the object and which the reflection. The quietness and peacefulness of nature which produce this result seem to have stamped the character of the people of the island with calm content. There is little if any of the hurry and worry and anxious striving for wealth that are to be seen in the large cities of the Australian continent. Tennyson must surely have seen Tasmania in a dream when he wrote the "Lotus Eaters." It is a land

> In which it seemed always afternoon—
> A land of streams,
> A land where all things always seemed the same ;

a land where,

> ——Sweeten'd with the summer light,
> The full-juiced apple, waxing mellow,
> Drops in a silent autumn night
> All its allotted length of days.
> The flower ripens in its place,
> Ripens and fades and falls and hath no toil,
> Fast rooted to the fruitful soil ;

a land where broad-shouldered, stalwart young men, six feet high, think it no shame to grow and gather raspberries, and drive their carts to market laden with the juicy spoil, and scenting the air with the aroma of the fermenting fruit, as it appeared to me, with a waste of manly energy, like using a steam-hammer to chip an egg; a land where then a heavy tax was put upon one of the necessaries of life (meat) in order that some few already overburdened with acres and golden wealth should live more sumptuously at the expense of their poorer brethren. It is a land where the atmosphere is so calm that thunderstorms—such as we see them here—are almost unknown. A native Tasmanian gentleman described to me the terror he felt when, on a visit to Australia, he first experienced one of those violent atmospheric disturbances.

And now the vehicle which carries the mails and passengers from New Norfolk to the Ouse dashes past down the steep incline to the bridge over the river. Luckily for me, time is not much thought of in Tasmania, and so the law punishes anyone who drives over a bridge at a faster rate than a slow walk. This gives me a chance of overtaking the driver, and having taken my seat, with a sick man—who occupied one whole seat, lying at length—and an old gentleman of good education and family, but very drunk, as fellow passengers, we wended our way up the beautiful valley of the Derwent. Here and there our road ran quite along the river's bank, where sweetbriar and hawthorn, and willows and many native shrubs, their branches bending over and dipping in the water, grow in hedge-like thickets. Now we leave the river as the road ascends the open volcanic downs of Macquarie Plains, and a most extensive view opens out to us. Collins' Bonnet, with its pointed sugarloaf peak, and Mount Field, with its little patch of perpetual snow, both rising some 4000 feet, are clearly seen. Far below we catch occasional glimpses of the river, its dark brown waters glittering in the sun's rays like polished bronze. We stop at various small hamlets and post-offices, and I am struck by the number of "mild-eyed melancholy," grey-headed old men who hobble out to gratify their daily curiosity in scanning the new faces of the coach passengers. They are the last remains of the old convict system slowly dying out. Now and then a bright-eyed, rosy-cheeked and fresh young girl—and all the Tasmanian girls are such—comes out with elastic step and beaming face to take the mail bags from our young and gentlemanly driver. He is a gentleman by education and birth and manner, and is evidently

very popular on the road. As young men of marriageable means and intention are somewhat scarce here, I do
not wonder that the fair maidens like to indulge in a little
innocent flirtation with our good-looking coachman.

The tipsy old gentleman, under the influence of the
bracing morning air, recovers himself. As I have known
some of his friends in another colony, and have heard
all about himself before, we become talkative, and
finding his unclouded brain is intelligent enough, we
have long and interesting chat about the old colonial
days, and the history and ownership of the country
we are passing through. The original proprietors of
the lands have all long since gone down in the struggle
of colonial life. The most of them seem to have been
official and military men under the old regime, and were
little fitted by early training for the hardships of the
bush. And so their places knew them no more. And all
this beautiful country, heavily grassed volcanic downs,
thinly timbered with the sweet-scented golden acacia,
has been inherited by the son of a tradesman. The misfortune of the grantees was his opportunity. The
tradesman, having the gift of acquisition, bought them
all out one after another, and thus formed one of the
finest freehold estates in all the colonies, containing
some tens of thousands of acres; watered by miles of the
river with the brown waters. My now sobered informant
was one of the last intruders who held his own lands
within the boundaries of this large domain. He, too,
was about completing a sale of his little property to the
omnivorous proprietor of the whole country side.

I learned from one little incident that the marriage-
market here is all in favour of the male sex. A sprightly
young damsel hails the coach from the roadside and takes
her seat. She informs us that she is leaving her place of
service in order to be married. I ask " if marriages are
frequent there." She tells me " No ; that the last one

was a year or more ago, when a young girl married quite an old man." I replied, " Are there any more young girls wanting to marry old men ?" With a sly look at my whitening beard, and with rippling, silvery laughter, she wishes " to know if I want a young wife, ' Seeing that I am already a Benedict, I reply somewhat evasively, but must needs express a hope that "if ever I am in that forlorn condition I may meet some one like herself." As she left us at the next village, wishing us a cheery " good-bye," I uttered a heartfelt wish that she might be happy with the man of her choice. I am sure she deserved to be so. Her good-humoured, cheerful presence, her sweet voice and her laughing eyes, that brightened our journey with their harmless coquetry, were, surely, enough to make happy her future home.

From this stage I am the only passenger, and after travelling some ten or twelve miles, reach the outermost limit of coaching traffic in that direction. The end of our journey was the little hamlet on the River Ouse. A blacksmith's shop, a small store or two, an old-fashioned two-story building, and a small church in the centre of a little graveyard, formed the habitations. The two-story building was used as a lodging-house. The magistrates had refused to grant a publican's license for it. Occasional tourists like myself stayed the night there, and now and then enthusiastic fishermen, hoping to catch that salmon which has never yet been caught, would take up their quarters here. A University Professor of Melbourne, enjoying his Christmas holiday, was even now with his rod somewhere in the neighbourhood. The streams that fall into the Derwent about here drain the lake district of Tasmania. The Ouse is a very pretty, noisy stream, with waters of a greyish-green colour, rushing along over a rocky bed through an open and fertile valley. Away up in this valley, which now lies in such peaceful seclusion, two wretched men, fifty-five years ago gave themselves up to justice. Afraid of each other, haggard and weary, ragged, sunburnt, and footsore, utterly tired of existence, after being the principal actors in one of the most terrible crimes in colonial history, they sullenly gave themselves up to the gallows as the only refuge.

Westward from this place lies Macquarie Harbour, some eighty miles distant. The intervening country was unoccupied, and is wet, mountainous, and thickly timbered. Five persons, named Broughton, Maccavoy, Hutchinson (*alias* " Up and Down Dick"), Coventry (sixty years of age), and Fagan (a boy), were serving colonial sentences at Macquarie Harbour, and were employed at an out-station under the charge of a solitary constable. Broughton, twenty-eight years of age, had, at eighteen years, been sentenced to death in England for robbery of an aggravated character. He had robbed his own mother, and his bad conduct had hastened his father to the grave. Of the last ten years of his life, most of it had been passed in gaol. Hutchinson had been a prosperous grazier, an owner of sheep and cattle, and of a run in the beautiful country between the rivers Clyde and Shannon in Tasmania. Nothing remarkable is known of the others. To obtain liberty under any circumstances was too strong a temptation to resist. The first attempt was made by Brougton trying to fell a tree upon their custodian. Broughton afterwards admitted this to have been a gross act of ingratitude, as the constable had been especially kind to himself. However, with some vague idea in their minds of obtaining their freedom, forgetful of the fact that the whole country was a prison from which it was impossible to escape, they bailed up the constable, and robbed him of all the provisions. This of itself was a cruel thing to do, for the man had no chance of relief for some days. Starting on their journey across the island, they seemed to have struck a due east course, with no defined scheme that could really lead to ultimate escape. Shortly, their provisions having been consumed, the four others agreed to kill Hutchinson. They drew lots, and the execution of the deed fell to Broughton. He killed him with an axe they had with them. They divided the body among them, carrying it with them and eating heartily of it. Hutchinson's body lasted them for some days. And now a terror of each other seized hold of them. The greatest jealousy prevailed as to who should carry the axe, and scarce one amongst them dared to shut his eyes for a doze for a moment for fear of being sacrificed unawares. Broughton and Fagan made an agreement that both should not sleep at the same time. While one slept the other kept awake. The fellowship of misfortune was completely ruptured by the accomplishment of crime. Hutchinson having been assimilated, three of them cast wolfish eyes upon Coventry. Fagan and Maccavoy proposed that as Broughton had been so successful with Hutchinson, he should perform the act upon Coventry. Broughton demurred, on the ground that he had already killed his man, and it was only fair that the others should put themselves upon the same level with himself. Some little sense of the force of this argument decided the matter. So Maccavoy and Fagan attempted to carry out the horrible business. The poor wretch, seeing them coming, cried out for mercy, and Broughton came not to his, but to their, assistance. Broughton now obtained possession of the axe, carrying it about with him by day and sleeping with it under his head at night. Before they had devoured Coventry, Maccavoy one night started up, and looking horribly, asked Broughton to go with him to set snares for kankaroos. They left Fagan by the fire, and went about 300 yards and sat down. Broughton had the axe upon

his shoulder, and was afraid Maccavoy wanted to kill
him, as he was the stronger. Broughton threw the axe
away, but farther from Maccavoy than himself, so that
he could reach it first. Maccavoy then wanted Broughton to kill Fagan. He refused, saying "he could trust
him with his life." They then returned to the camp,
where Fagan was warming himself by the fire.
Broughton threw down the axe. Fagan looked up and
said: "Have you put any snares down, Ned?"
Broughton said: "There are snares enough, if he did
but know it." Broughton sat beside Fagan, Maccavoy
on the other side sitting with the axe close by, looking
at them. Broughton lay down and was in a dose when
he heard Fagan scream out; he leaped to his feet in a
fright, and saw Fagan lying on his back with a dreadful
cut in his head, Maccavoy standing over him with the
axe in his hand. Broughton said: "You murdering
rascal, you b——y dog, what have you done?" Such
a phrase from Broughton's lips, all things considered, is
at least remarkable. Maccavoy said: "This will save
our lives," and then struck Fagan another blow on the
head with the axe. Fagan only groaned after the
scream. They stripped off the clothes, and after quar-
relling about the shirt they cut up the body in pieces
and roasted it, as it was lighter to carry and would keep
longer, and was not so easily discovered to be what it
was. Two days after they saw native-dogs catch a
kangaroo. They got the kangaroo, and threw away
the other flesh. In two more days they gave themselves
up at Maguire's Marsh, at a hut belonging to Mr.
Nicholas, near the junction of the Shannon and Ouse
rivers. Soon after, these two died on the gallows.

Of Maccavoy little is known. Broughton's career
presents a curious psycological problem. He seems to
have been utterly without conscience or sense of obli-
gation. During the few days allowed to him before

his execution he spent his time ·in execration and blas-
phemy, and threatened to kill the clergyman, the Rev.
Mr. Bedford, if he dared to speak to him.   His belief
in a Supreme Being was confined to his using His
name with the foulest of language.   He stated he had
never entered a church but once, and then to steal the
poor's box.   A few minutes before his death he at length
admitted that Mr. Bedford was the only friend he had
ever known.

And so the terrible story ends, duly attested by
J. Bisdee, whose duty it was to take down the sickening ·
details from the mouth of Broughton, who made a
request that the whole should be published.

Sketches of Country Life.

A CATTLE MUSTER IN THE HILLS.

THE station was situated on one of our chief western rivers, among the high mountain ranges through which that river runs, before it finds its way into the great interior plain. In the bed of the river there are long broad reaches of deep and never-failing water, in which fish of almost fabulous size were caught. I knew of some that weighed over 70lbs. The water, as it meanders through a dense grove of native oaks, and seen from the highest points of the hills some hundreds of feet above, reminds one, as it shimmers in the midday sun, of a band of bright silver set in a lining of dark green velvet. Nature never makes mistakes in her colouring. High and precipitous mountain ranges rise sheer from the water's edge at the outer angles, and less abruptly from the narrow alluvial flats which skirt alternately opposite sides of the stream. Their steep sides are somewhat thinly timbered with white box trees, with their pearl grey metallic looking leaves; growing from amid rocky masses here and there stand the bright green currajongs. On their more sunny brows dark patches of the sour oak show in great blotches. Their summits are frequently fringed by the useful stringy barks, and their somewhat stony soil was covered with the luxuriant kangaroo grass. Among these hills, some of which are of volcanic origin and fantastic shape, having great walled battlements frowning like fortresses of old Titanic times, there roamed a large herd of wild cattle. These are the cattle we are intending to muster, for gold has been found in Australia. The finding of the hundredweight has been made known throughout the world. The Turon gold field and Bendigo and Ballarat are in full swing. There are thousands of fresh hungry mouths rapidly landing on our shores, and these animals roaming on the hills, from being almost useless, are now worth money, worth at least a pound for every crown of their value before this fresh human influx.

Before commencing to muster, I must go back some thirty years further in the past in order to tell how these animals came to be among these hills. In the year 1821 and within the County of Cumberland in New South Wales, at some little distance from a main road, a neat picturesque cottage stood, surrounded by an orange grove. Sweet smelling honeysuckle and jasmine and cluster roses were trained along and hung pendant from its verandahs. It was a curious oldfashioned place, rambling and planless. Commenced with a building of two rooms of wooden slabs, lath, and plastered, as the settler's family increased and his means improved, various additions on differing levels, having great thick walls of rubble stone and earth, were made, with a general result that with long, low verandahs and narrow passages, and unexpected steps (pitfalls to the unwary) we have a very quaint, but very cosy and comfortable human residence. All around the house, and quite close to the eaves, stood fine large, dark green orange trees. covered with veritable fruit of the Hesperides. On the side of a hill, stretching over some acres behind and beside the cottage, a plantation of the same pleasing objects was to be seen. In front, on a gentle slope towards the watercourse, was a vineyard, probably planted with some of those vines (or their offshoots) which the Gosport waggoner (told of in "My Grandfather's Pocketbook") delayed to carry. As oidium and phylloxera were not a trouble in those days, the vines in that virgin soil were in due season loaded with fruit.

To sit and hold social chat in the shade of the verandahs, in the warm languid air of the early summer, amid the scent of orange blossoms and the drowsy murmur of bees, to be tended by the gentle daughters of the house bringing rich ripe oranges in profusion, argued an Arcadian simplicity of life very pleasant now to look back upon.

Quite at the rear of the house were placed the usual sheds and stables of such a farm, and among the necessary articles there was a grindstone, at which a young lad of sixteen was busy sharpening an axe. Idleness was not allowed here.

"William," said my grandfather to this lad, his son, "How would you like to go over the mountains?" His eager face lit up as he replied at once and without hesitation—

" There was nothing he would like so much."

The mystery of the blue hills of the west, which were plainly visible from the highest point of the orange orchard, had at length been solved. Such of the early settlers as found favour with Governor Macquarie had already wended their way with their small flocks and herds into the new fields of the Bathurst downs. After much delay it had come at last. Many repeated applications had been made by our colonist to be allowed to join in the exodus to that promising land. No favorable reply had been vouchsafed, until Governor Brisbane ʻguided our destinies. A license to occupy some of this rich pasture land had come at last. Many wistful glances during years of hope deferred had been cast over the distant summits of those blue hills before the permission came. We are not slow to make use of it. In February, 1822, a few hundred breeding ewes, some horned cattle, one mare named " Sally," a loaded bullock dray, and some convict servants, under the direction principally of the young lad, started on their arduous journey over the Blue Mountains. Some sixteen days were occupied in the passage of the hills, over which the railway now passes in half as many hours.

Bathurst Plains at length reached, our settlers located themselves on the western edge of the open land, built the necessary huts and yards, and patiently awaited the arrival of the surveyor to define their boundaries. The Government at that time reserved all the land lying to the west of the Macquarie River for the use of their herds of cattle. These were depastured at various places near Bathurst and Wellington. The herds numbered a few hundred head each, and were tended by men on foot, one man to each hundred head. It was the duty of these men to muster and count their charge daily. All private settlement was confined to the east bank of the river, where the larger grants of land were made. So when Mr. Surveyor McBrian came and measured lands for Messrs. Cox, Hawkins, Piper, Icely, and Rankin, 2000 acres to each, our people with their right to 320 acres were pushed out of their location, and had to seek for another field. They thought this hard at the time, but it proved to be of much ultimate benefit, for from the fresh coign of vantage a large area of waste land was available for the increase of the stock. The blacks were troublesome at Bathurst in those days —the cause, very frequently, was their ill-treatment by the whites. Poisoned dampers had been left purposely exposed in shepherds' huts in order to tempt the blacks to steal and to eat. They did eat, and died in horrible agony. No wonder reprisals took place. Our hut was one day surrounded by a large party of blacks, fully equipped for war, under the leadership of their great fierce chief and warrior, named by the whites "Saturday." There were no means of resistance, so my father, then a lad of eighteen years, and alone on the premises, met them fearlessly in the door. He spoke to them in their own language, in such a manner as not to let them suppose he anticipated any evil from them. They stood there, sullen, silent, motionless. My father's cheerful courage and friendly tone disarmed animosity. They consult in an undertone, and depart as suddenly and as noiselessly as they came. The next thing known of them is, that they killed (was it not just retribution?) all the men at a settler's place some miles distant—the very place where, it was rumored, the poisoned bread had been laid for them. This place is called the "Murdering Hut" to this day. After this business, with that peculiar sense of justice which has not rendered our dealings with the inferior races a source of much congratulation, the extermination of the tribe was decreed, and almost completely carried out. They never molested either man or beast of my father's. He had proved himself their friend on previous occasions, but if at this time he had shown distrust or hostility, they certainly would have killed him.

The cattle having increased, more room and better

F

pasture is desired for them. I find a receipt in my grandfather's pocketbook for the purchase of fifty-nine head of Government cattle for £300 in the year 1826. In 1805 he had bought his first cow, an old one, from Captain M'Arthur, for the sum of £65—"she proved a bad bargain." It was understood at this time (near 1830, I think,) that the Government were about to sell all their cattle and abandon their stations. One of these was situated near the place described above, and not far from the junction of the Macquarie and Cudgegong Rivers. We watch for the abandonment and take possession as the Government cattle are driven away. The pasture there being very nutritious, within twelve months a small draft of fats are sent to the Government stores at Bathurst. An astute old colonist sees the cattle, and learning where they come from, "jumps our claim" with a number of land grant orders. So we " shift our hurdles" a few miles, to the place about which I write. The men who have charge of this station and herd are assigned convict servants. I have very kindly and pleasant recollections of these old servants. I was not taught to look upon them as depraved people. Their honest fidelity, their watchful care of their master's property, their interest in his affairs, was quite sufficient to wipe away all stain of previous misdoing. They always spoke of his stock as "our cattle, our sheep, our horses," and looked upon the whole business as a partnership concern in which they were quite as much interested as the " cove " himself was. My father, "the cove," had a peculiar method of dealing with these servants. When any of those who were entrusted with his property came to the "farm," as the head station was called, he always took them by the hand, held long friendly talks with them about their business and duties, listening attentively to everything they had to say. In fact, he always treated them as free and honest men.

This behaviour instilled into them a feeling of self-respect, which did much for their benefit and reclamation. Straitforward, industrious, and faithful, the highest wages you give now-a-days cannot buy such unselfish devotion. When we recollect that many were sent out for the most trivial offences—"for stealing guinea-pigs off hen-roosts," as they somewhat facetiously, and not always unfairly, described their crimes —no wonder many of them turned out well and became good colonists. Three at least of my father's servants were utterly innocent of the crimes for which they were transported. The innocence of one was so proved to the satisfaction of the Government that a free passage was given him and his family back to Ireland. Another, one of the best all-round farm servants he ever had, was sent out for " stealing a goose." The papers charged him with no more. His explanation was, that one night, in a silly freak, he threw a stick among some geese feeding on a common; unluckily, he killed one. Foolishly he carried it to his cottage gate, leaving it on the road. Discovered in the morning (he did not deny placing it there), he was convicted and transported. An industrious, honest man. He had left a young wife and little ones behind ; the chance of ever seeing them again was so hopeless, the iron of unmerited disgrace, too, had so entered into his soul, that within twelve months of his arrival, he pined away and died of a broken heart.

I yield to no one in my admiration and tender regard for the fair sex, but candour compels me to say that I believe that if our dear old friend Mrs. Poyser ever had been a colonist, in those days, at least, she would have told us that the ladies of the transport system were generally much more than " made to match the men." The attendant of my childhood, for whom I have the most tender recollections, was a kind, gentle, utterly guileless

old man, who led me by the hand, gathered wild flowers
for me, "he hath borne me on his back a thousand
times," guarded my every footstep, and, I feel sure,
loved me as his very own. An infant brother was
entrusted to the charge of one of the ladies of the
period. One day, during the absence of her master
and mistress, she neglected her duty, and when they
returned, their accidentally drowned dead child was
all she had to show for her womanly care. Such was
the difference, as it appears to my recollections.

My father's righthand man in the formation and
management of this station was Jonathan ——. Old
Jonathan, as I always knew him, was a man of very dis-
tinctive character. He had been a poacher in his youth;
had been caught in the act, and was banished in consequence to this country. He was a very stout, strongly-
built man, with a determined and almost ferocious cast
of countenance. Very reticent, his hut mates used to
complain that he would not speak to them for days at a
stretch ; a most faithful, trustworthy, industrious, honest
servant, who fully proved his fidelity, even to risking his
life in defence of his master's property. His first duty
after his assignment was to watch his master's orange
orchard, one of the very first ever planted in the colony,
and just then coming in full bearing. Oranges were then
worth half-a-crown a dozen wholesale in the Sydney
market. They were worth stealing. One night a party
attempted to plunder this orchard. They came fully
prepared *in puris naturalibus*, and had oiled or greased
their skins to prevent their being held. Jonathan, with
his dog and bludgeon, were too much for them, putting
them completely to the rout, but not before one of the
slippery scoundrels had made a considerable flesh
wound with a knife on the body of his assailant. Such
fidelity was rewarded by promotion to the responsible
position of head stockman over all the cattle, then in-

creasing largely in numbers. Shortly after his establishment at the station, a bushranger named " Killalee,"
made his appearance in the neighbourhood. This class
of robbers was composed of rather poor creatures, who
perhaps because of a hard taskmaster, or because they
disliked work, preferred a roving life in the bush to any
kind of industry. Their principal depredations were
raids upon the ration bags of their fellows at the out-
stations. They could make no greater hauls, for money
was scarce, and was certainly not to be found in stockmen's and shepherds' huts. This man knew of
Jonathan's determined character, and considered it
would add a feather to his cap to rob him. With a
flavor of chivalric fairness, he sent word to Jonathan of
his intentions. " If he comes here to rob me," said
Jonathan to the messenger, " I'll shoot him." Killalee
did come. Both Jonathan and his hutkeeper, old Jerry
—a faithful, courageous old Irishman—were at home.
Jonathan was sitting on a large meat-block near the
door of the hut, lacing up his boots. He either did not
notice, or did not care to notice, the bushranger, who
brushed past him through the door, and entering the
hut, found himself at once in the firm grasp of old Jerry.
A struggle ensued; they fell on the floor, old Jerry
playing the part of " under dog," " Killalee" losing his
pistol in the struggle. Jonathan, hearing the row,
looked round, and taking in the position, walked into
the hut, and obtoining possession of his gun, took aim
at the thief. Having been a poacher, he was always a
keen sportsman and good shot, and his gun was ever
ready. " For God's sake don't shoot," said old Jerry,
" you'll shoot me." Old Jerry still hugged his man, as
Jonathan, saying " Shoot you! be d——d," pulled the
trigger. Nearly exhausted, Jerry slowly rises, shaking
from him the dead body of the bushranger. On due
inquiry, the authorities justify Jonathan. Killalee's

intention was to seize the fortress—and but for Jerry's vigor, a very different end of the story might have been told. Killalee had a number of friends waiting in ambush close by, who ran off at their chief's defeat. This shooting had the effect of breaking up a gang of incipient desperadoes, a part of whose plan was the murder of a whole settler's family, the head of which had had some of them punished.

Jonathan, on another occasion, led a party of police to a lonely hut, where he knew some of these men were harboured. As they drew near the place, he counselled "rushing" the hut, so as to take the inmates by surprise. He, when the time came, gallopped up to the door ; arrived there, he looked round for the police. They had gone the other way ! Jonathan was fired at, but missed, by the gang. Finding he was deserted, he turned his horse's head and rode slowly away, muttering curses at the cowardice of the police, whom he did not further seek.

My childish awe of Jonathan was much heightened, not only by this story, but by a fellow-servant of his once telling me with bated breath that " Jonathan was an atheist." What sort of creature this was I could not conjecture. I could only gather from the mode of telling that it was something too dreadful for further explanation. If Jonathan was an atheist, it is strange that he showed some superstitious feeling with regard to this killing. For Killalee having been buried near the hut, Jonathan would not remain there, but removed the station to another part of the run. It was always understood that he did not like living too close to the bones of the dead bushranger. Killalee's body was, many years afterwards, disturbed by a party of diggers seeking for gold. The metal was discovered in somewhat rich quantities just under his grave. Such is the irony of fate. He was buried in that, to obtain a little of which dishonestly, he probably lost his freedom and his life.

The time was now arrived when Jonathan, from increasing years and bodily infirmity, must give up his charge; so his master sends a young man as his successor. When he introduces himself, he is scanned slowly from head to foot. "Ugh! Only a tailer, by——," says Jonathan, "merely this and nothing more." Not another word passes till the next day, when the station horses are brought up to the yard. "Ugh!" says the old man, "take that horse and come with me to get a bullock to kill." They ride silently for some miles, till an undulating table land, lying behind and beyond the tops of the highest hills, and called the Kangaroo Ground, is reached. The wildest cattle on the run are here. A mob of some thirty or so is seen, which Jonathan guesses contains what he wants. They dismount and tighten their saddle-girths. "Ugh!" said Jonathan, " I'll take the first turn out of them. I want to shoot them down that leader into the creek. The main camp is there," which means that they are to drive the cattle down a long sloping ridge into the valley nigh a thousand feet below. His mate nods acquiescence. They ride on again as noiselessly as possible, trying to prevent even their horses' footsteps from being heard till they obtain such a position behind the cattle as may compel them to run the way they desire. The mob lying in camp are roused either by the scent or sound of the approaching horsemen, and jumping suddenly to their feet, give one startled look around, and race off as fast as they can gallop. The country is rough, scrubby, and stony, but Jonathan is ready, and before the wild creatures are fairly on their legs he tightens his reins, and giving his horse a sharp reminder with his doubled stockwhip, is racing after them. He passes and turns them, and then slackens speed to see how his mate be-

haves.   The mate does the right thing, at which
Jonathan gives a grunt of approval, for as the mob rush
towards him, he meets them at the proper point, and
they wheel round and dart off again towards Jonathan.
This zig-zag process repeated soon brings cattle and
horsemen to the brow of the range.   The cattle do not
like being pressed over this range, so the horsemen
close upon them.   Here a great brindled bull shows
out, and with head erect charges at them.   He will
not be denied, and as he makes good his escape, his
companions steady themselves and look anxiously and
eagerly after him.   That is the road they would also
like to go.   " D—— him," roars Jonathan, "that is an
old game of his.   Stick to the rest."   So, with whip
and shout, they dash at them and fairly force them over
the top of the range and on the edge of the long spur.
Now comes the time for discretion and judgment, for
coolness and decision are wanted here as much as
in matters of far greater moment.   The cattle race
down the hill, making stones and dust fly again.   They
look to right and left every yard they go to see if there
is room to break away.   It is a long and steep grade
down to the valley.   There are many loose stones and
reefs of rock cropping up in that wild course.   The
thing to be done is to jam on one's hat, stick in the
knees closer to the saddle, gather up the reins in a short
grip, and let the horse choose his own footing.   Fix an
eye ever on the cattle, and keep on racing level with
their quarter, and if they show the slightest sign or
attempt to break away, give them a rattling volley with
the stockwhip.   The leader of this mob was a large jet-
black stag, or bullock, without a single white hair ; his
skin always had a satin sheen upon it.   They were good
horses and daring riders who could keep time with
" Saturday," as he was called, in memory of the old
aboriginal chief.   It is not every horse that knows how

to extend himself in full gallop down these steep inclines. I have ridden many there. I never had but two under me that managed it perfectly to my satisfaction.

Well, Jonathan and his mate racing on either side keep the leaders straight, urge on the laggards, check at once the breakaways, and so at length reach the valley and a broad alluvial flat, on which is the main camp. The animals, with their flanks heaving, their tongues hanging out, their sides bedewed with sweat and slaver, must be "rounded up" here. The pace has been so severe that cattle and horse cannot stand it much longer. So Jonathan signs to his mate to draw rein, while he gallops round the mob. His mate's experienced eye soon discerns the camp, and as the cattle come whirling round towards him, he keeps wide of them, and by degrees turns them towards the great currajong tree that marks the stopping-place. The mob, completely blown, ring up under this tree and consent to stand. Then Jonathan rides up to his mate, beckons him to dismount, as he does himself, loosens the saddle-girths (the poor horses are blowing like steam-engines, and the sweat pours off them in streams), takes out his pipe, fills and lights it from his tinder-box (matches were a thing of the future), draws three whiffs, and thus breaks silence gruffly, "Ugh! Give me your hand, young fellow, you're no tailer, by————." So he recognises a worthy successor in the daring mountain rider, who, in that wild race, could keep pace with himself. Your veritable stockman of that day had a profound contempt for men who were only capable of minding cattle after they had been captured, that is, to tail them, but had not go enough "to run them in" from the ranges. When the animals regain their wind, the mob is started for home, the cattle completely cowed, and allowed to gorge themselves (which they

do greedily after their long gallop), with water at
the creek, now jog along quietly enough to the
stockyard.

Then Jonathan, who for years has been a free man
and earning wages, gives up his charge, and his master,
as a reward for long years of faithful devotion, determines
to allow him a pension for the remainder of his life.
Before fixing upon the amount, medical opinion is
obtained, and the old servant is pronounced to have but
few years of life in him. So a hundred a year is settled
upon Jonathan. Annuitants are proverbially long-
lived. Our pensioner immediately marries a young
wife, and renting a small cottage and garden from his
old master, lives happily and comfortably for many
years, until upon a day he strolls out to see how a tree
he was burning down for firewood is progressing towards
its fall. As he approaches the tree it does fall, its outer
branches striking him to the ground. He is much
bruised, with collar-bone probably broken. He endures
the pain for a few days, then tells his wife " he can bear
it no longer." So taking down his loaded gun, as his
terrified wife, unable to prevent him, rushes off scream-
ing to her neighbors some half-mile away, with
deliberation he puts the muzzle to his head, and
manages somehow to discharge the piece. When the
alarmed people arrive in haste, old Jonathan lies calm
and still. Poor old Jonathan! Poor old Jonathan!
Not for all the wealth of the Indies would thy kind old
master have had thee commit this act of violence
against thyself. A fierce, determined man he lived, a
fierce, determined old man he died. He was one of
those of whom the best and most was not made in this
world. Such faithful courage and force of character
were worthy of a better education and a higher sphere
than fell to his lot.

Another of these old servants, and for some time a

hut-mate of Jonathan's at this station, was old John Pool. Partly because I know of no one who could feel hurt at it, and almost wholly because of the last bene-volent act of his life, which deserves to be written in letters of gold, I feel no compunction in giving his full name. When I first knew him he had obtained his freedom and worked for himself, principally as a shearer. He sheared in my father's shed, and for years occupied the same corner. He was almost wholly un-taught, and of rather penurious habits, so much so as to be quite a proverb among his fellows for " close-fistedness." He was transported on the evidence, and the only direct evidence against him, of a little girl. He himself used to tell the story of " how he was lagged," how he and some of the lads had broken into a shop and were taking the goods, how they were disturbed and ran away, how the little girl in court swore posi-tively to him, and only to him, as the one she saw through the glass door at the back of the shop, and by the light of the thieves' own lantern. Having got so far in his story, John Pool would give a little laugh and say, " Ees! ees! she swore 'twas I;" and then he would look on the ground, as his mind carried him back in reverie through the long years and over the weary seas to the scene in the court, with the little girl holding fast to her story in the witness-box, and all resentment, if, indeed, he had ever felt any, having died within him, he would say, with a sigh, " Poor little gal, she wur right, too; she wur right, too." So long as old John Pool lived here not the slightest act or thought of dishonesty could be made an accusation against him. For many years before his death he did nothing else for a living but shear sheep during the season. He lived with an old shipmate in a small cottage on my father's property, where he occu-pied himself in cultivating a small garden of fruit and flowers and vegetables, all for the benefit of his friends. He was very fond of flowers: roses and pinks and wall-flowers were his favorites, and whenever he had any in bloom, he invariably carried one in his mouth. I have known him shear sheep all day long, and, day after day, with a rosebud pendent from his lips. The pictures of Lord Palmerston in London *Punch* as the "judicious bottle-holder" with a flower in his mouth, always reminded me of him. I never knew old John Pool to be drunk, or his lips to utter a foul or blasphemous expression. The purifying influence of his wall-flowers and roses had their refining effect upon his manners. It would have been too inconsistent for the lips that delighted in carrying rosebuds to have been guilty of such impropriety. His close and penurious habits enabled him to save a considerable sum of money. At his death, except two very small bequests to old fellow-servants, he left all to the Bathurst Hospital. Since his death, some sixteen years ago, the Institution has drawn from his trustees the sum of £1578 11s. 7d., and will receive annually for the future some £150. As this sum is doubled by the Government subsidy, no wonder the directors of the hospital revere the name of old John Pool; for though rich men of their abundance have cast much into its treasury, they are far and away distanced by his posthumous charity. One provision of his will is characteristic of his old English heart. " I specially" (specially, mark you,) "direct my trustees to purchase on every Christmas Day one glass of the best port wine and a sufficient quantity of good plum-pudding for every one of the patients for the time being in the said hospital." The odour of his blameless repentful life was fitly savoured by this his last benevolent act. He did his " level best " to make such ample amends to the world for the one solitary breach of its rules as to make one hope that his spirit, " never regretting its roses," lies quietly with—

> "A holier odour
> About it of pansies,
> A rosemary odour
> Commingled with pansies,
> With the rue and the beautiful
> Puritan pansies."

I am not a little pleased and proud to be a trustee of his estate, for, among many other kind offices, he was one of my first instructors in the art of shearing a sheep.

After Jonathan's supervision came to an end, the herd of cattle we are going to muster became very wild; They had become so valueless from a limited market, that it was hardly worth while to pay men to look after them. The discovery of gold changed all this. So the quieter and more manageable were gathered together, and had been driven away to the vast fattening plains of the interior.

On my leaving school, this station, with its remnant of wild " scrubbers," was given into my charge. Seeing that these brutes are utterly useless where they are, I gather together four or five lads of my own age, all sons of old servants and born and reared on "the farm." We run in a lot of unbroken colts from my father's paddocks, bit them, saddle them, and at length tame them sufficiently to start for a muster. While I have been at school trying to understand the theoretic properties of the conic sections, my young companions who remain at home have been practically learning to solve the problem of how not to describe a parabola with a horse's head in one of the foci. Their practice is more successful than my theory.. I mount my colt, and like some bodies which describe hyperbolic divergent courses, show a disinclination to complete the orbit by not returning to the point of departure. Not to put too fine a point upon it, I get " bucked off." They stick to their seats like very centaurs.

Ah! how much would I not give now for one month of my youth and the wild enjoyment of that first experience of life in the bush. It was the springtime: plentiful rains had fallen; the hills were covered with the beautiful sweet-scented kangaroo grass, and were as green as a young wheat field. Every watercourse had a little stream trickling down it. The river was broad and full. How delicious the "campings out," with my companions, on some little alluvial flat, in a pretty valley deep-set among the hills; the green grass, knee high, for a bed; a large spreading river oak for a canopy; the music of the gurgling stream; the gentle sighing of the night wind through the trees for a lullaby. No anxiety to trouble one. Our only care to circumvent the wild animals we hear bellowing around us on the mountain sides.

So I lay me down to sleep, with my saddle for a pillow, not without tender thought, maybe, of a fair-haired stately maiden, who seems as distant and unapproachable as yon bright and nearest star, a fitting emblem of purity and wedded love, pointing ever to the Southern Cross! "How unintellectual! and how rheumatic!" "Don't you believe a word of it, my dear sir, or madam." A solitary commune with nature in her wildest moods by mountain range or river bank leaves no soul untouched with higher aspirations. Much physical endurance and courage is required in the life I describe, and manliness and resource are undoubtedly developed. As for rheumatism, I have suffered more from an open window in a luxurious Sydney club than I ever felt after months of sleeping on the ground in the open air.

Well, to make a long and tedious story short, after many such races as that described with old Jonathan, after many hairbreadth escapes from charges of wild bulls, from horses falling (tumbling heels over head in fierce gallop in such rough wild country, scarce a day passes without temporary disaster to man or horse), we do manage by stratagem and hard riding to capture some hundreds of these wild cattle and transfer them to better pasture, where they grow into great, weighty beeves, and bring in much profit.

Is there any place in New South Wales where the same wild exhilarating life can be enjoyed now? The whole country is fenced in, and the gentle merino crops the tender grass on the hill sides, and utters his plaintive bleat where the rocks resounded to the bellowings of the great wild bulls fighting for the mastery.

Will the national character alter with the more gentle occupation? I sometimes think, as universities are desirable to keep up the standard of intellectual excellence, so some wild exciting outdoor life is necessary to keep us up to the mark in animal courage and endurance. Whale-fishing and explorations in search of new country, and rough ridings such as I describe, were once outlets for superabundant and adventurous energies; but these fields are now all closed. After this muster is finished, I look upon my youthful education (such as it is) as complete. Having with painful study stammered through Virgil and Homer, under the preceptorship of my ever dear and kind old friend, the Rev. Dr. Woolls, I now know (in addition to all cattle-craft) how to shoe a horse, bake a damper, and, on a pinch, wash a pair of moleskin trousers at the river side.

We all remember how Sir James Martin, some years since, threw the words of Jesus, the son of Sirach, at Sir John Robertson, "Can wisdom be found in those whose talk is of bullocks?" Sir John, when our Premier, had boasted at a dinner at some country place that he could still "run in a bullock off a mountain."

I recollect how my heart warmed to the old man for

that simple bucolic confession, and thought how he might have capped the quotation by another from the same wise author, "Hast thou cattle? Have an eye to them, and if they be for thy profit, keep them with thee."

How much of Sir John's straightforward manliness and indomitable courage, that never struck a fowl blow, that never said a spiteful thing against a man who was precluded by his very position from answering, that never allowed himself to be made the vehicle of the spite and slander of others, that in short

"Nothing paltry does or mean,"

is due to his early initiation in the wild bush-craft such as I have endeavoured to describe above, is, I think, not much of a matter for conjecture.

When once you have learned to take your stand in a cattle-drafting race, and not flinch at a wild bull's charge, but with your stick deftly give him a facer in the forehead that does not kill but lays him stunned and sprawling at your feet, you may perhaps become a wicked man; but I venture to think you will never be a mean or unmanly one. This kind of life, I am sorry to say, is being completely civilized out of the country, at which I can only exclaim, "The more pity! the more pity!"

A CATTLE MUSTER ON THE PLAINS.

WHEN gold was discovered here, all those who were the owners of sheep and cattle stations thought at first that ruin stared them in the face. Flocks left to starve in the yards, or wandering at will through the bush, the prey of native dogs, herds left uncared for, was the picture that presented itself. Employers felt that no wage they could offer would induce men to serve them when the temptations of the goldfields were so great. For a time there was much inconvenience. A shepherd I know was famishing with the "cursed thirst," and had actually picked up a nugget as it lay exposed on a sheep path. He showed it to the overseer, who, true to his master, told the shepherd it was only a piece of old brass, and threw it away, and cajoled the old man to wait a little longer. A rich Sydney merchant and squatter visited the goldfields with a country friend living in the vicinity. On the way he boasted that his men would not leave his property uncared for. Curiosity compelled them to stop at the first mining claim they came to, and there was the squatter's managing overseer and a party of his former servants at work. As the men had just about satisfied themselves that their claim was a "duffer," a fresh bargain was made, and they returned to their allegiance. But men of this class, who had tolerably good lodging, easy times, and plenty to eat, soon found that gold-getting was a very uncertain and uncomfortable way of earning a living. Employers, too, awoke to

G

the fact that an increasing population meant higher
prices for their produce, which enabled them to give
wages equal to and better than the average earnings of
the diggers. Sheep-farming in those days was not a
very widespread industry, and was almost wholly confined (in New South Wales, at least,) to the western
slopes, where married men and their families were
employed. The wife and little ones took charge of the
sheep, while the fathers tried the diggings, and shortly
satisfied themselves that that was not the life they preferred. So things righted themselves, and the unmanned
farms and stations soon had their complement of
labourers—when meat and flour were almost at famine
prices. Fat cattle, from being worth 30s. per head,
became worth £8 or £10; wheat, from 2s. per bushel,
rose as high as £1. The greatest rise in the value of
fat stock took place in Victoria. The report of the
high prices at length reach us in New South Wales,
and as we have a cattle-station some 400 miles north
from Melbourne, on the Lachlan, in the year 1854 we
determine to fit out a party to muster a mob of fat
cattle, and drive them to that city for sale.

Calico tents were not known here before the diggings,
and were just then coming into use. My mother and
the ladies of the house make such a tent for us. The
imagination of one lady is much stirred by the idea of
the adventure. She is a late arrival from England, but
has lived much on the Continent, and being somewhat
self-willed, would defy conventionalities and make one
of the party. It is not without keen disappointment
and tears from her that we depart without her. We
travel down the valley of the Lachlan, enjoying, as
young men could in those days, the camping out and
the freedom of the life. The journey passes without
adventure, save that, one morning, the leader of the
party is so ill with measles that we must stay. A

couple of days' spell, a dose of salts, the universal remedy in those parts, procured after riding some five miles (there is no doctor within a hundred), with wild duck broth to follow, soon puts our patient in travelling condition, and we leave a very pretty romantic camping place within a horseshoe lagoon, under the shade of gigantic blue-gums, and knee-deep in green grass.

The station where the fat cattle are is reached after a ride of 300 miles. The station hut is a small one, built only for the accommodation of the stockman and the hutkeeper. The latter was an old soldier, and as there is plenty of pipeclay in the river, and neatness and cleanliness had been well drilled into him, the little dwelling is tidy and natty within and without. The hut is built of round pine saplings, with a bark roof. There is no ceiling, so the ventilation is perfect. There are two or three small rooms used as sleeping places, built round one large apartment used as an eating-room. The fireplace at the end is large and commodious, with great logs on blocks on each side, so that the men may sit round the fire in the cold winter nights and smoke and yarn. At mealtime damper and beef are the only fare, washed down with great basins of tea. Cups and saucers and yeast-made bread, an innovation of female civilisation, came years after. When bread so made was first offered to the station blacks, they eyed it suspiciously, tasted it and spat it out, and offered it back, contemptuously declining to eat it, as being "too much like it that one wool." The river, swollen by the winter rains, ran sluggishly by, close under the hut. At a few yards distant is the blacks' camp, as several of them are employed to help with the cattle. They get new suits of clothes occasionally, blankets, tobacco, and as much as they can consume of bread and beef and tea. When meals are on they come to the door, and their share is cut off for them by the hutkeeper. The camp is a merry place, and notwithstanding its uncomfortable squalor, cheerfulness and silvery laughter reign supreme. The gentle, good-natured Boney is there, with soft hands, tapering fingers, and filbert nails, which, if white, were shapely enough to be the envy of the most refined of drawing-room "dandies;" and Jackey Beecham, a thin, wiry lad, with a prematurely old face, whom no horse could throw. He seems, when at full gallop, to ride his steed all over like a monkey. Alban also is there, a young man from the wild tribes, just learning to say a few words of English, and discovering that clothes and food and a horse to ride are preferable to the life nature has provided for him. Poor fellow! He was to copy the vices of the whites, and years after kill his mate in a drunken row, and learn what prison life meant.

There are several blacks there with their wives. The most notable among the ladies is Maria, *alias* "The Soldier," Jackey's mother. She had her musculine nickname from her majestic walk, and tall, upright figure. She "stepped as does an Andalusian barb." A Roman empress, full of the pride of royal beauty and of imperial power, could not have moved with a more graceful and dignified freedom. She could swim like a duck, too, and once in time of high flood had saved the life of a young gentleman whom she saw upset from a canoe in mid-stream and like to drown. She dropped her opossum's fur cloak—her only garment—from her shoulders, and posing on the bank but for a moment, a splendid, nude, and breathing bronze, she plunged into the water, and, swimming out to him, seized the half-drowned lad, and landed him all gasping, but alive, on the grass at his father's feet. Wet and glistening, she donned her cloak, and wringing with her hands her dripping hair, squeezed the water from it, with much shouting of "Yuccai!" ("Oh dear!") and breathlessness and cheery laughter. Poor daughter of the plains! with natural instincts for her only rule, she risked her life to save that of a fellow mortal. An act so sublime, and performed without any sense of dutiful guidance, but from an innate feeling of unselfish helpful pity, put her at once on a level superior to most. The very last time I saw her, worn down with disease, the fruits of her environment, she was nursing, with placid endurance, and tending as best she could under sheets of propped-up bark, a poor aged sister, blind and helpless, and slowly dying miserably, with much querulousness and peevish groaning. At times Maria could scold in her own tongue with rapid speech and flashing eyes, and foaming mouth and clenched hands. In youthful fun I did something to anger her, and engaged in a wordy contest with her. I was fresh from school, and as she screeched at me in Wirradgerie (which would not bear interpretation), I answered her with Greek and Latin (Homer and Virgil) in accents of sneering contempt. I flattered myself the victory remained with me, but it was not till I assured her, with as much derision as I could command, that she was no better than a "Doctor Johnson." Her vocabulary of vituperation being exhausted and herself utterly breathless, and seeing from my amused expression that I was only "chaffing," her good humour returned, and her heart being without malice, shrieks of laughter, from both sides ended the vocal war. Boney's sister Nelly had not the decided character of Maria. She was remarkable for her shapely hand and arm, soft and rounded, her large, dark, splendid, lustrous eyes, her even ivory teeth, and her sweet, musical, melancholy voice. If Nelly had only been washed and dressed and cared for and made sweet she would have passed as a beauty even among her white sisters,

These people who fill my early memories of the

" Great Plain " with kindest recollections are nearly all gone. A mound of earth here and there slowly and surely sinking to the common level, with adjacent trees scarred over with deep-cut markings, rude armorial bearings, are all that will remain to remind us that they ever were. It has been the fashion to decry them as being the most degraded. When we consider the natural meagreness of their surroundings, that life with them was a continual struggle ; every meal had to be hunted for ; that, except the dog, there were no animals to domesticate, no natural plants capable of cultivation to supply a store of food, and, added to these, a climate so genial as to call for little exercise of ingenuity, it need not surprise us that they were not more advanced. In character they were very human. They were never vulgarly intrusive. I never knew one to be purposely offensive in manner. Civility towards them always ensured respect from them. They were splendid mimics. I have seen them in their corroborees, act the part of white men having peculiarities, to the very life. They had a large fund of common sense, and seldom said or did foolish or silly things. I have seen them exhibit great love and affection for each other. Two young men were very great friends. " Whispering tongues had poisoned truth," and a sudden enmity arose which blood alone could wipe out. They faced each other with weapons of war. The most dexterous sent his spear through a part of the body of the other. Honor being satisfied, the victor gave himself up wholly to nurse his old friend and late enemy. It was very touching to witness the kind attention that anticipated every want, and the admission that they had both been in the wrong. If the mischief-maker had made his appearance then, I fancy he would have had a bad time. So far as crime and immorality are concerned, with the revelations of our own courts before us, I doubt if we are justified in throwing any stones at this unfortunate race, to whom we have given more vices than virtues.

Before we can muster our cattle we must inform our neighbours of our intention, and seek their help. The nearest lived twelve miles off. He was a stockman and managed a herd of cattle. Old Bill W———— was the very chief of his order and profession. A North of Ireland man, he came out when young " on his own hook." Some of his family had emigrated before him. His boast was that he was the only one of his name who had brought money with him to the country, and now he was the only one without it. Bill thought this was more to his credit. He was a middle-sized, thick-set man, with stooping shoulders. He had black coarse hair and large grey eyes, and true Celtic countenance, and moved awkwardly. Wiry and weather-beaten, and full of unresting energy, though not a good rider, he was almost always in the saddle. His great delight was to wander about over the great ocean-like plain with a neighbouring stockman and a blackfellow, (camping out night after night) seeing where the cattle were. If Bill had a failing, it was a love of rum, of which in his time he had, so he said, " drank as much as would float a seventy-four, and he hoped before he died to drink as much more." He was a sure prize for the travelling hawkers or " bumboat men," who were illicit sellers of spirits. His occasional debauches never rendered him unfit for his work. He had a wonderful constitution, and was never ill. His immunity from sickness he attributed to the rum. He always marked Sunday with a clean-shaved face and shirt and trousers as white as a black gin could make them. The only religious ceremony I ever knew him to engage in was to stand godfather to the half-castes that came into the world in the neighbourhood. Bill was strictly honest, and with him honesty meant everything, and in his belief, atoned for everything. His master trusted him implicitly, and the trust was not misplaced. When you shook old Bill's great rough misshaped hand—a hand deformed by hard work—and received his growled greeting, always accompanied by a gruff laugh out of the depths of his great hairy chest, notwithstanding his faults and his vices, you felt that you grasped the hand of a man with a character worth studying. His common sense and strong will always ensured obedience from those he had to deal with. He could knock more work out of both whites and blacks than any man about, and during musters all round that neighbourhood, by tacit consent, Bill's advice directed the plan.

We attempt to muster within Bill's domain. We gather a large herd of cattle together ; the rain falls in torrents; the country becomes a great quagmire; we give up the task, and starting for home, during one wet night, we are all lost on the desolate plain, and ride about aimlessly, hoping in the dark to stumble across a tree. At length, near morning, we come to a clump of trees. It is proposed to light a fire, and it is discovered that the whole party possessed just one wooden match. (Vestas had not been invented then.) To provide something inflammable portions of our dress are contributed, and with anxious ceremony the match is struck; it lights, and joy! We soon have a large log blazing with fire, around which, completely tired and worn out (having been continuously in the saddle for some twenty hours), we throw ourselves on the soft wet ground and sleep till daylight.

After a few days, as the weather cleared, we made another attempt, and as some twenty men, whites and blacks, gather together at a friend's station some fifty miles distant from our own on the river, we again start off from this fresh point of attack to search the great plain for the cattle. We know that all the herds are gathered together and mixed indiscriminately in the back country. We are now in Big Jack's boundaries. He is the stockman manager of the B—— station, and has just brought his young wife into that part. A tall, slim, pretty native girl, with an aptitude for house-keeping. All the young fellows in the district (as she is the only white woman there) believe themselves to feel a tender regard for her, just that chivalrous sensibility that comes of sex, and has its civilising softening influence, and nothing more ; for the wife herself is pure and gentle, and Jack is popular, and is, moreover, a rough customer, and any attempt at undue familiarity would be resented by her and meet its due reward from him. As we ride out across the plains, we come to a pine-covered sand hill where the wild blacks have killed some cattle during the time of the rain. This they managed by following on after them, and tiring them out on the heavy wet ground, and then, getting close enough, sticking spears into them. And they gorge themselves with the meat, and rub the fat all over their bodies, and hold hideous revelry at night in the fire-light, their bodies marked with white lines, looking like skeletons and deaths-heads, and they dance in measured time to the clashing of war implements, with their limbs quavering.

We camp here under the tall straight beautiful pines that grow only on these small sand islands, and divide into groups, instinctively congregating according to social order. We make beds of the pine leaves, but before we sleep there is much smoking of tobacco, and general "yarning" about old times and late trips to the large towns of Sydney and Melbourne, and of the sprees held there, and there is much talk of bullocks. As the great fires of the sweet-scented burning pine logs crack and roar, and send up showers of sparks and bouncing coals, and light up the trees with dancing and ever-changing wavering light, songs are sung and stories are told not quite fit for religious tea meetings, and although verging at times on the indelicate, as a rule, substantial justice is done to virtue an morality in the strains. The men are mostly young and virile, and there is a rough, manly animalism about the scene that comes of young and energetic spirits, and the independence of the wilds that if not very refined, is at least ruggedly picturesque. That these men are there at all shows enterprise and love of adventure. For at that time this place was on the very outer rim of colonial life. No white man lived anywhere in the country beyond that blazing camp fire. The blacks start after the horses as soon as daylight begins to show. As hour after hour passes without their return we become anxious, but while away the time in athletic exercise, leaping and jumping. From the games played there then the place is called the " Jumping Sandhill" to the present day. As noon passes by without the horses, I climb up to the top of the highest pine. I have a most extended and lovely view over the wide expanse around. Away on the horizon I see some black specks, which at first I suppose to be low bushes. I watch, and as I notice them close up and open out in evident motion I know them to be the blacks coming with the horses. Far away and all around I see small white objects. These are some of the cattle we want. The view of the ocean from the South Head at Sydney always reminds me of that sight from the head of that old pine. Suppose all the surface of water seen from those cliffs to be thinly grassed land, then one can form some idea of the appearance of the great Lachlan Plains. The crests of the waves, as here and there they lazily break in foam, will represent the white cattle scattered over the waste. As the day is too far gone to muster, we break up the party and camp in different places that night, so as to secure good positions for the morning's attack. We agree to meet at a certain place with all the cattle we find.

That night we watch our horses. We are mounted and start off before sunrise. The party I am with soon come in sight of cattle, and we see drove after drove scattered over the plain between us and the level horizon. We canter along for miles, starting each drove as we pass to run in the direction of the rendezvous. As on all sides we see clouds of dust rise both above and below the horizon, we know that our mates are as busy as ourselves. In the cool brisk morning air it is a spirit-stirring scene. The great fat bullocks, with their heads and horns upraised, race off at our approach, their clattering hoofs sending up clouds of dust. As the numbers we have started gather nearer together, we close upon them and direct them in a long straggling column to the meeting place. The old bullocks take the lead in ponderous and ungainly gallop and heavy, swinging trot, their tongues lolling out, from which the saliva pours in glistening strings, covering their necks, briskets, and sides with flakes of foam. The rear of the drove is made up of cows and calves, bellowing and bleating in deafening chorus, and moving more slowly in dense compact body, so that in a short time our cattle form in long, dust-raising procession—a many-coloured moving mass, red and white and pied. We all assemble with our droves, which number some 3000 head or so, all roaring and bellowing. We boil our pots for the dinner's tea, run down a calf and kill it for meat, and soon fillets of veal, still quivering and transfixed on short wooden spits, are being roasted before the fires, and filling the air with an appetising odour, and are eaten with and on great slabs of "dam-per," and washed down with copious draughts of milkless tea.　After this indigestible meal is over, the business of cutting out the bullocks is proceeded with. A certain number, those on young horses not used to the work, gallop round and round, keeping the cattle in the same spot ; the rest ride fearlessly in amongst them and select the fat bullocks wanted, and drive them out singly from the mob, and make a smaller drove some hundreds of yards away from the main lot.　The cleverness of the old stock-horses at this business is wonderful.　When once they know that the rider has determined upon cutting out a certain animal, they will turn and dodge after it with great intelligence and rapidity. A slight pressure of the knee, a touch of the heel, the least turn of the rein with the wrist, is a telegraphic signal instantly understood and obeyed.　Sometimes they are quicker than the rider, knowing by watchful instinct what should be done, as an unwary horseman may learn to his cost ; a sudden stop and rapid turn as the bullock dodges, often unseating him.　So the bullocks are compelled to leave their mates.　The noise of the cattle, the gallopping and shouting, and not unfrequent blasphemous execration and cracking of the long whips by the men, the constant stream of fat bullocks racing off to the select mob as they are " cut out," make a scene full of life and activity.　All the fat bullocks having been run out, they are taken by some of the party to the nearest station on the river, where they are kept in custody until the muster is completed.

Some nine or ten days pass as described above, when our mob, numbering some 600, is gathered together, and we start for Melbourne.　Our way was down the River Lachlan to Booligal, and thence across the " One Tree Plain " (so called because of the splendid gum tree growing by itself some nine miles from any other of its kind, and making a landmark seen at a long distance) to the Murrumbidgee.　We swim our cattle over this river at Lang's crossing, now called Hay. The brothers Lang—Gideon, the doctor, and William—owned Mungadal, on the south bank. We watch our cattle every night as we go, two and two, with horse in hand, walking or riding round them all night. In the daytime we drive them along at a feeding pace over the plains, walking behind them and keeping them straight for their destination. Not a panel of fence anywhere interrupts our march over the country. We reach the Murray in due time, at the hostlery of James Maiden, the working man who made a fortune and lost it in a pastoral speculation. The last time I saw him he was walking and carrying his swag. I was glad to extend hospitality to him, and pass the evening in talking over old times. He was independent an self-reliant, and would accept no favours from any one. When he lost all, he bravely shouldered his kit and walked off to seek honest employment. For such a sturdy character one must feel respect.

We drove our cattle to the old saleyard in Elizabeth-street, and sold them at an average of £10 per head for the whole 600, some pens selling as high as £17 per head. Melbourne was a small place then, compared with the present magnificent city. We put up at the old Saracen's Head, in Bourke-street. When we arrive we are in full bush costume. We secure bedrooms and go down town and purchase fresh suits of clothes, more becoming; and then to a large bathing establishment, and leaving our old, rough and soiled clothes there, appear at the inn in our new coverings. A friend whom we meet advises us to change our lodging to the Port Phillip Club Hotel. We call for our bill, and learn that there is "no account against these gentlemen." We have to explain that we are the stockmen of the morning, and our fair hostess, laughing merrily over the mistake, graciously consents to accept our money.

We saw the most charming actress, Mrs. Charles Young, perform in the old theatre in Queen-street. In duty bound we fell head over ears in love with her. We came back to Sydney in the old steamship "London," and bought another station with the proceeds of the sale.

PAST AND PRESENT, AND TWO TRIPS TO THE DARLING RIVER.

MY grandfather took off his hat. He dashed it on the ground; he then jumped upon it. After the performance of this sublime saltatory sacrificial rite, with bared head and uplifted face, he was about to raise his voice on high, doubtless in pious ejaculation and invocation of the gods befitting the great occasion, when my grandmother plucked him by the sleeve.

"My dear, my dear," she said, "do not be so foolish."

He had a most tender regard for the sex as a whole, and a most reverential affection for his wife in particular. In his estimation she ought to have been—and so far as his sphere was concerned she was—queen of the universe and high priestess. Every word from her had all the force of law and of a divine oracle. She was wholly worthy of his regard. When he lost her, after nearly half a century of supreme marital happiness, as he recalled her determined and loving perseverance, amid all their early trials, and these were neither few nor light, he insisted, with tearful repetition, that " She never despaired ! she never despaired !"   Once only in her letters, written at the darkest period, when her husband was treated as a rebel by those he knew to be rebels, unjustly cast into prison, several of her children struck down by severe illness, and the responsibility of providing the daily meal thrown upon her, does she show any repining.   His delicate regard for the sex was once shewn in a superlative degree.   He was doing some work in his shirt sleeves, a condition not unusual in this sultry clime.   In that predicament he was suddenly called upon to answer a letter from a lady.   The opening sentence of his note expressed an apology for the coatless state in which the urgency of immediate reply compelled him to write to her.   Surely apologetic gallantry could no further go.   It was a charming sight to watch his rapt and devoted expression when having said "farewell" to a lady at his door, as she tripped lightly away, he would follow her retreating figure with eyes beaming with a pure and holy regard, and gently exclaim, " Pretty creature ! pretty creature !"

The hat was sacrificed in consequence of a temporary disruption of an old friendship.   A friend and near neighbour was the fortunate owner of a horse, a very scarce and envied possession in those days.   My grandfather was the lucky possessor of of a small library.   The loan of a book for the loan of a horse was a fair and equal bargain, to the mutual delight and advantage of these old settlers who were then pioneering the County of Cumberland.   A message had been sent by the horseowner to borrow a volume.   My grandfather, momentarily irritated and out of temper by something not at all connected with his friend, answered somewhat testily, "If your master wants to 'read my books tell him he may come and read them here." Shortly after this, some occasion of importance called the man of books to Sydney, so he sent a request for the loan of the horse. "You tell your master," was the reply, "that if he wants to ride my horse he may come and ride him here." Disappointed at such an unexpected refusal, what could he do but smash his hat? His wife plucked his sleeve, and then sliding her fingers down his arm took his hand in a soft caress, and looked at him with compassionate surprise, not unmixed with amusement. The electric circuit was complete, equilibrium was established, the storm passed away, and Christian serenity following, the old amity was restored. Friends were too few and far between in those days to be recklessly cast aside. That friendship was renewed is certified from the fact that a daughter of the horse-owner, dying many years after both the old friends had passed away—an aged and much respected ancestress of numerous descendants, in her last moments, at that time when memory will carry us back to the days of our childhood and early innocence, blotting out in kind oblivion much that we would forget—"babbled" continually of her father's old friend. His name, in kind remembrance, was one of the last upon her lips.

My grandfather pioneered the County of Cumberland, not with flocks and herds, but with pick and axe and spade, the veritable implements of the service; cutting out of the long-standing forests of ironbarks and blue-gums an opening wherein to build his cottage and grow crops and plant orchards to support his young family. I learn from some of his written memoirs "that in 1804 he had made some progress in the clearing and cultivation of the farm at Baulkham-hills, and had planted the orange, which, with due attention to its treatment and health, became productive and profitable. Soon after we went (in 1801) to the farm the orangery was commenced. My father's friend, Colonel Paterson, presented me with three young orange plants he had brought from San Salvador (Bahia?) They were the first orange trees planted at Baulkham-hills, though I had planted and raised many lemon trees from seed. The lemons were at the time of our arrival in the colony (in 1800) worth 2s. per dozen, but I do not remember seeing any ripe oranges till years after. In six years some of my own trees had a few oranges, and in 1807 I sent loads of them to the Sydney market, then held in Charlotte-square, or place. They were sold at 2s. 6d. per dozen to the fruit-dealers in Pitt-street." With respect to other cultivation he writes:—" About this time (in 1804) we had very fine seasons, rather moist than dry, the crop of maize very abundant, and affording food for man and horse, Indian corncakes and doughboys were in general use, and proved wholesome and nutritious. For several years the wheat crops had suffered from blight and rust, so much so that we began to despair of its being a wheat country. The rust was thought to proceed from the nature of the soil, having so much ironstone in it" (*sic*). "In the fine crops of maize bountiful nature made ample amends."

The following extract tells in simple and expressive language of the difficulties and privations the old colonists had to endure :—" I had always regretted, as did my beloved wife, the want of good schools and education for our numerous and industrious family. We each did what we could to teach their young ideas how to shoot, and keep them in a right course, in prayer and love of the Creator, and of industry and virtue. Early, too, our boys were obliged to tend the ewes and cows. Though we had assigned servants, they were too expensive, provisions and clothing being then high in price. I had known fresh beef and mutton as much as

2s. 6d. per ℔., and flour the same. Tea and sugar, so
essential to English comfort, were generally very dear.
Wheat and maize, after the great flood (1806?), were
five pounds per bushel. Lemon leaves were at one
time substituted for tea, which had risen to £6 (six
pounds) per pound, when it was said there was only one
whole chest in Sydney. Governor King left the colony
in a wretched state of famine, partly occasioned by a
succession of floods in the Hawkesbury. When
Governor Bligh arrived, he had great difficulties to con-
tend with; much distress and disorder was caused by
scarcity of food at the Hawkesbury. The suffering of
the settlers was very severe. The Governor ordered a
number of the Government cattle to be slaughtered
every week for the supply of the families there with
fresh beef, and thus many valuable lives were preserved. Governor Bligh in this showed his humanity,
as he was a man who feared God and honoured his
King. A poor woman in Sydney with four children,
applied to him for food. He said, 'I must put you on
the store.' She said, 'This is Tuesday, and I cannot
wait till Saturday, and my children have been without
bread two days.' The Governor rang the bell for his
steward, and told him to give the poor woman what
bread there was in the house. He said, 'There is very
little,' so the coachman was called, and told to give her
a bushel of corn from the stable."

In 1812, our pioneer had to part with his books to pay
off a debt contracted while in England on the Bligh
business. The sacrifice he made in that cause, I venture to think, must be reckoned with before Bligh's
thorough condemnation can be accepted. He had
nothing to gain, but everything to lose, and did lose and
suffer both in person and pocket by his adherence. As
I remember him, he was a sturdy, independent character—no courtier of those in power, but with most

perfect self-respect; always trying to do what was right, because " to follow right is wisdom in the scorn of consequence." The parting with his volumes was a great grief. He had a perfect passion for books and for collecting them. He could no more pass a book-stall without stopping to turn over its volumes than can a confirmed drunkard pass the place of his dearest idolatry. Where are those dear old stalls that added picturesqueness to the streets of Sydney forty years ago, with their loads of precious, rusty-looking leather bindings, and presided over by civil, melancholy old gentlemen in spectacles, who were always poring over some of their own treasures? I remember one in particular where, as a schoolboy, I snatched many a transitory joy. It stood somewhere in Lower George-street.

> " All, all are gone—
> The old familiar faces."

My grandfather was among the first to prove the successful and profitable cultivation of the orange—an industry that has since grown to be of national importance. His sons were among the early pioneers of the western country. They felled trees, thus clearing their lands, and grew crops and planted orchards and established sheep and cattle stations on the waters of the Macquarie, the Bogan, and the Lachlan between the years 1822 and 1842. In this last year a station had been formed on the Lower Lachlan, 400 miles west from Sydney. It was stocked with a herd from the station managed by old Jonathan. Down to the year 1857, and for some time after, squatting was almost entirely confined to the lands permanently watered. No one thought of settling on the back blocks. The possessors only of the frontages had taken up some of the country contiguous to their riparian holdings. These primitive, genuine old squatters had no idea of improving .the country by securing water and by fencing. Their cattle stations were managed by a stockman and a hutkeeper and blacks. They were not speculative; they had no great overdrawn bank accounts; their wants were few, and they lived simply and unostentatiously, and exercised a kind and wide hospitality. There were no inns in the pastoral districts, so every door was open, and every respectable passer-by was a welcome guest. Once a year, perhaps, they journeyed as far as Sydney when the wool or the mob of cattle got down. The wool was very frequently carried in their own bullock drays, The wealthiest of them travelled in one-horse two-wheeled gigs. Time was no great object in those days. Things went slowly, as though people expected at least to live a thousand years. About three days and a-half was the time occupied on the journey from Bathurst to Sydney. I sometimes meet in the streets of Sydney a jaunty, erect, very youthful-looking old gentleman, with jet black moustache, who recalls with vivid recollection journeyings in my boyhood over the Blue Mountains. He was the most popular host on the road. His inn was on a low eminence. Quite close ran a mountain stream. Around and over the large granite boulders strewn in its bed there rushed, in joyous and refreshing cadence, and beneath the dense shade of oaks, whose

" Songs are steady harmonies,"

a constant, copious stream of crystal water. At that elevation, nearly 3000 feet, the air is pure and cool and brisk, like good champagne to flat beer, as compared with the atmosphere of the lowlands. After being rattled and jolted and jumped and bumped, with much jarring concussion, over the rough-stoned road, down the long grade, in the great lumbering mail waggon, and thundered over the bridge across the stream, and gallopped up the gentle incline, with loud cracking of the long coach whip and shoutings by the driver, and the horses were pulled up at the door, all breathless and steaming in the keen frosty morning air, you were sure of the cheeriest of welcomes. The fresh boiled eggs, the crisp buttered toast, the juicy mutton chops, the bacon and eggs (inevitable dish), the hottest of tea and coffee, with unlimited milk, spread on the whitest of table linen, allayed with much satisfaction an appetite of such sharpness as can only be acquired in that wholesome region. The first mails were carried over the mountains on foot. Gangs of convicts making the roads were stationed at intervals in prison-like stockades, and guarded by soldiers; the soldiers, in relays, carried the mails.

The old road was not without its romances of fatal accident and crime. There was the unfenced, fearful precipice at Lapstone Hill, over which a loaded wool-team (neglected by its driver, who had stayed at an inn to drink, the horses proceeding on their own responsibility), had fallen, dragging down horses and all in frightful wreck into the valley below. There was the lonely culvert near the summit of Mount Victoria, under which was hidden the murdered body of a woman—her only fault that she had trusted too much; his only motive to be rid of her. There was the embankment down which the mail coach had tumbled over and over with its passengers, who had refused to walk past the unsafe spot at the earnest entreaty of the driver, and had met death or injury in consequence of their foolhardy obstinacy. There was the great frowning mountain, up the face of which some of the early woolgrowers of the Bathurst country had to roll their bales inch by inch until the summit was reached, and the incline to the seaboard. There were the convict gangs and their red-coated guards, forming the road, the chains of the prisoners clanking as they worked: a scene happily blotted out for ever. There was the rounded, grassy, thinly-timbered hill near Springwood, where my father and his black companion camped for dinner in the days when few inns, if any, were established on the western road; when his black, in frightened accents, adjured him not to stay, as a whitefellow had been murdered there. He had too surely discovered some charred remains in an extinguished fire. The perpetrator and the victim alike remain unknown to this day. As I speed over the hills in the luxurious railway car, I am tempted to wish, if only for one journey, to re-establish the old hostelries, to revive the old hosts, to bring past and present into direct comparison. Laud as we may our advancement in the comforts and conveniences of civilization, early colonial life, with its continual calls upon self-reliance, had more colour in it in the old days. While we have gained something in artificial æsthetic refinement, we have lost much in natural rugged picturesqueness.

The time came at length when the hereditary pioneering instincts (if I may so call them) claimed their exercise in my own person. In 1857 our attention was directed to the unstocked condition of a greater part of the Darling River. The diggers had rendered no longer tenable for pasture purposes the country lying between Bathurst and Mudgee, a large portion of which we had held for nearly five-and-thirty years under sheep and cattle. The remnant of our flocks must be removed to fresh fields. Some runs were secured fronting the Darling. It was necessary the country should be seen. After a few hours' notice, I was ready to start off for that then remote region. A friend accompanied me as far as the Lachlan River, where I was to meet two other friends, who were to be companions on the trip. We left Bathurst in the month of May, 1857, and passed the first night at the then small village of Orange, in

the very farthest inn to be found in that direction
towards the west.   Orange then was near the boundary
of what was known as the settled districts, all beyond
was held on pastoral tenancy.   In the crisp air of the
early morning, passing the Canoblas mountain covered
with snow, we followed an unmade track through the
indigenous forest, our hearts light and joyous with the
unrestrained independence of bush life.   Our path was
very solitary and unfrequented.   We call at a squatter's
station ; we are hospitably entreated (as was usual) to
stay the night.   Our host is a splendid specimen of an
English gentleman, bringing British pluck and energy
with him to carve out for himself a fortune in the wilds
of Australia.   Handsome, bluff, and hearty, he could
have masqueraded as Henry VIII., with most accurate
"counterfeit presentment."   A brother-in-law of John
Sterling and F. D. Maurice, and incidentally mentioned
by Carlyle in the "Life of Sterling," it was a privilege
in a land unhallowed by great associations, to know a
man bound by such ties to such names.   He has
travelled and seen much, and with clear intelligence
delights such "home-keeping youths" as we were
with much instruction and pleasant discourse, Our
cultured hostess, tall and slight, moves about and
orders her household with quiet, graceful dignity. One of
the very salt of the earth, she behaves with such charming
condescension and extends such kind hospitality to us
as to fill us with pleased surprise and gratefal recollection.   Our national character and civilization will
owe much to that cheerful and heroic self-sacrifice which
sends such refined and cultivated womanhood into our
wildernesses to make them all the better and brighter
for their presence.   Australian mothers, discourage not
your daughters from cheering the void spots with their
sweet enlightenment.   A great and patriotic work has
to be done, and all honor to those who can cheerfully

fulfil their duties in this regard with noble self-denial and unregretful refusal of the social gratification of city life.

Leaving this home, then, with its picturesque aggregation of cottages in early Australian architecture, its shaded garden walk of trellised grape-trees (the elsewhere vines had in that rich alluvial soil become great as trees), its cloth-of-gold roses, and its kindest hospitalities, ever after to be one of the greenest spots in our grateful memories, in due time we reach the valley of the Lachlan, and pass the place where the town of Forbes now stands. No human habitation stood within miles of it then. I noticed that some hopeful solitary digger had commenced a prospecting shaft there and abandoned it. Five years after, gold was discovered there. Right under that very shaft the richest claim on that field was found. That unknown man was within 100 feet of fortune. Perseverance, and a mate to assist, and in a few days a great reward might have been his. At that time no gold had been got nearer than 100 miles from this place, and with the limited practical experience of that day it seemed a most unlikely one to contain it. Was it imperfect, instinctive foresight or blind stupidity that prompted this abortive clueless search for hidden treasure that really was so near? Years after, the diggers were induced to sink and search for it here because a small quantity had been found on the surface of a hillside close by.

A story of this goldfield shows how romantically Fortune deals out her favours. Two poor young men, brothers, landed in Australia and wandered as far as the Young gold mines when the news spread of the discovery of this new field. They went there in the first rush, secured a claim, and in a few weeks' time took out of the earth some £10,000, and sailed away again for England. How strange! Two poor men wander

12,000 miles to a spot of ground a few feet square in the heart of Australia and take therefrom a fortune and return again the way they came, having been absent from their friends no longer than a holiday's outing.

The valley of the Lachlan is a rich pastoral land, subject to drought and floods; feasts and famines alternate there. I have known the rainfall to range from 10in. in 1867 to 42in, in 1870. The climate, from April till October, inclusive, is perfect in its bracing geniality. The river is a narrow deep ditch. Its banks are fringed and its course marked with very large blue gums, *eucalyptus rostrata.* Among their trunks and branches imagination may see numberless fantastic figures, and trace out here and there semblances of gigantic gothic architectural arches and designs, Myall trees and salt-bush abound in the flat plains through which the stream winds its way. High rocky masses are occasionally seen, the more hardened remnants of a great formation long since carried away atom by atom, and showing the denudation that has been going on. At this time very few, if any, of the leaseholders on the Lachlan resided on their stations. The properties were managed by servants, and the whole of the country was occupied as cattle runs. The only improvements were the rude slab-walled, bark-covered huts of the stockmen, and the yards necessary for working the cattle. For the frontages, and extending about five miles back from the river, only was any rental paid. The back country was used as a common by the frontage proprietors. In the winter the cattle wandered into the back country, and when the shallow waters there dried in the summer, they found their way again to the more permanent river. Now, in 1887, the whole of the country, both river frontage and that lying behind, is all fenced and under sheep,. and tanks and dams innumerable have been constructed. All the best lands have been sold at £1 and more per acre, and holdings for which the owners grumbled to pay a few pounds per square mile rental to the Government, now pay many of them £50 per square mile when the interest upon the capital freehold value given for them is considered.

We travelled down the river, camping out night after night, until we reached the station formed for my father in 1842, and situated nearly 300 miles west from Bathurst on the eastern edge of the great, almost tree-less, level plain. Across this plain lay our path for 220 miles to the Darling river. Except on the Lachlan frontage, this stretch of country was quite unstocked, now it is all fenced and improved and under sheep.

This plain is one of the greatest gambling tables in the world. Many fortunes have been won and lost upon it. One man begins the game with tens of thousands of pounds in his pocket, and in a few years retires by the courtesy of his banker with nothing more to call his own than the clothes he stands up in. Another, with very little capital, tries his luck with the very same property, and in a few months sells out with a large fortune at his credit. And so the game goes on—the players are sanguine and eager, and the stakes are high. As the rainfall ranges from a very few inches up to feet per annum, as the price of wool varies from 6d. to 1s. per lb., so the luck alters in like proportion, Feast or famine, fortune or beggary, is the general rule. There is a fascination about this plain very alluring to young energies. Independent of mercenary considerations, one cannot ride out upon its great silent solitudes, with its oceanlike level horizon all round, without a weird feeling, very taking to the imagination. A human being is a mere atom in the centre of its wide rings. One's heroism is stirred, and he feels how dull and tame city life is, with its daily monotonous round, while nature here in solitary grandeur is to be warred with and made subservient to men's uses. Some such thoughts passed through my mind as I kept my watch by the camp-fire. Our party consisted of four whites and one black. Our camp for the night was on a low sand-hill, covered with hop-bush scrub. It stands like an island in the level waste, and had been visible on the horizon for hours before we reached it. There is a small morass close by, where the wild blacks have scooped out a small hole, and then filled with rain water. We were about 100 miles from everywhere. The wild tribes had been here lately, as we learned from the heaps of grass straw scattered about, from which they had threshed the seeds. The grains are ground between two stones, a primitive pestle and mortar. As the process of trituration is carried on, water is sprinkled on the mass. When the whole is reduced to a thin batter, it is then eaten raw, being thrown into the mouth from the forefinger. As the blacks may still be in the neighbourhood, for more abundant caution, we decide to keep watch. We pitched our tent and made luxurious beds of the grass straw. We gathered a great pile of firewood of dead scrub, for the nights were chill, and the cook required a good heap of ashes in which the damper for the morrow's meals must be baked. We went to bed early, feeling that our little camp was but a mere speck in the centre of the great circular waste that in the dark imagination pictures as reaching to the very stars. The only sounds are the gentle murmur of the fire, the tinkle of our horse-bells, and our blackfellow's not unmelodious chant, which he keeps up for an hour or more with rapid and monotonous cadence. This at last becomes intermittent, and as sleep asserted itself, ceases, and

"Night and oblivion reign over all,"

except the man on watch, who occasionally startles us from our slumber with noisy replenishment of the fire. We immediately pray for the repose of his soul somewhere. Mine is the morning watch, and the duty to boil and bake the day's provisions. I am called betimes, and find myself standing alone, with the great dim solitude around me. I fill a bucket with water. The dark pool, with the stars reflected from it, looks like some wild thing with a supernatural power in its great apparent depths. I spread out a leather sheepskin on the ground, and put on it some pounds of flour, I make an inverted cone in the centre of this heap. I sprinkle some salt over it, and pour lukewarm water in the depression. I gradually mix the "ingridiments," taking care not to " drown the miller," and then knead the whole into a homogeneous mass of stiff dough. I pat it out into a circular cake about half an inch thick. All the while the fire is leaping and flickering and murmuring in pleasant companionship. Of all natural religions fire-worship is the most rational. I must kill my little deity, however, and make use of his dying remains. So I make a smooth place among the ashes and cinders, and drop my cake upon it with a flop. A cloud of ash dust in revenged spite, is dashed up to my face. I cover the dough with ashes and cinders, and wait the result. I make another fire to keep the meat-pot boiling, and then, with firearm thrown over my shoulder, I march about, a solitary sentinel on that lonely sandhill. I feel altogether heroic and sublime, and repeat lines of Tennyson (a new revelation and gospel to me) about Arthur and Bedivere and Galahad—words of the sweetest and purest of all English singers, who teaches the lesson that man may be courageous and manly, though he be not steeped in vice and impurity. A scent of burning flour reaches my nostrils, and I tumble headlong from my mental exaltation, and learn that poetic reverie makes a bad baking.

The daylight begins to show glow above, with light

yellow streak and roseate on the level horizon, and as the light increases the little birds, of which there seem to be countless numbers perched in the low scrub, commence to chirp and twitter, and the bell-horse rouses and stretches and shakes himself, ringing his bell violently, and settles down to his early feed of grass hitherto uncropped. The morning mirage begins to show itself. Distant objects, trees and hills, and the level plain itself below the horizon, seem uplifted and hang in the air, and in imagination I saw dark weird stretches of water and frowning fortresses and rocky precipices and fanciful landscapes, such changing and chaotic shapes do common objects take in the early dawn. But all soon "fades into the light of common day." There is a midday mirage on these plains very different from that of the early morning. In this, near objects seem to be removed to great distances; solitary trees that are near appear to be miles away, and are like ghostly shadows of their realities. Glassy pools of water show themselves quite close, and great shining lakes are seen on the horizon. But it is all illusion. As you advance they alter in character and recede, and at length, as the sun declines, they disappear.

I call the black and start him after the horses. I put on the fire the pots of water to boil for the tea, and call the rest as

"The sunbeam strikes along the world"

with

"Calm, still light on yon great plain."

The country we rode over was quite in its natural state. The grass was thin and bunchy, saltbushes in places growing very thick. We left the open plain and passed into a thickly-timbered scrub, when half our journey was over. The soil was a soft red loam, and our distressed horses at every step sank in over the fet-

locks.   We rode in Indian file in order to mark a
distinct pathway for our return.   We crossed the tracks,
quite plainly to be seen, of an emu, a dog, and a
blackfellow, the first evidently hunted by the two last.
We started an emu from his nest (the male bird sits)
and took the thirteen eggs.   We passed a night and a
day at the pretty romantic-looking Mount Manara, with
the roofs and rocky walls of its caves stained in
coloured pigments, with the marks of the blacks' hands
and feet.   At this place, a few months before our coming,
a party of our friends from the Lachlan had returned
discomfited.   One was dangerously and others seriously
wounded in their sleep by a night attack of the black
tribe of the place.   We watched, but saw nothing of
these enemies.   Two days more of travel through
country covered with rich herbage and grass, and
timbered chiefly with mulga and spotted tree, brought
us to a lagoon full of water, evidently supplied by
the river.   Across a narrow plain to the west we saw
the fringe of high blue-gums which marks the presence
of a great stream.   Our stock of meat being exhausted,
we shot for our breakfast.   I secured a very small
parrot, and found grilled parrot on damper to be not a
very unsatisfactory meal.   After breakfast we gallopped
over the plain to the high trees, and there, to our
delight, was the River Darling, running nearly bank
high, a narrow, but deep, sullen, sluggish and disco-
loured stream.   Anxious to find the newly-formed
station of an old friend, we travelled down the river,
and, of course, went wrong.   That night we camped
on a splendid sheet of back water from the river, and
cooked the day's sport for supper.   Ducks, pigeons,
black and white cockatoos, mutton birds, and—no! not
old crow, here we drew a sumptuary line—stewed in a
bucket, all mixed up " in one delicious gravy," made a
banquet fit for the gods.   From a half-civilized black,

who comes to our camp, we learn that our friend's
station is up the river, and on the opposite bank.
Arrived at the place called Caulpaulin, we were ferried
over the swollen stream by an old black lubra, one of a
large tribe camped here. Our boat was a frail bark
canoe. I waited till the last, and saw my friends disappear over the top of the bank as the canoe was brought
back for me. A surly young fellow took the place of
the woman. In midstream he suddenly stopped pad-
dling, and glared at me and growled gutturally, "You
got him 'bacca?" I do not smoke; but realising the
poet's saying—that "one touch of nature makes the
whole world kin"—I hurriedly replied, as we seemed to
drift too rapidly down the stream, "Oh, yes; plenty
'bacca." He was satisfied, and a few vigourous strokes
brought us to land. He had evidently taken a mean
advantage of the position. I do not think he knew
another word of English.

The next day (not being unused to such canoes) I
paddled myself over the river. The paddle was a rough
stick, and the exertion was not light. When I reached
the bank, the old gin of yesterday was there, and at
once noticed a small stream of blood on my hand; a
sharp knot on the paddle-stick had torn the skin. With
an unfeigned expression of deepest sympathy saddening
her features, she snatched the stick from me, and at
once applied her teeth to the offending part, which by
this means she removed. As she handed it back with a
grateful look in her large dark eyes, thankful that she
had been able to render me a service, I was much
touched by her action, and recognised in her sympathetic kindness the truly divine compassionate instincts
which ever distinguish womankind and make them to
be of one universal sisterhood. I doubt if ever

"Dear George Eliot, whom I worship daily,"

and who everywhere in her writings preaches with

much insistence the doctrine of self-sacrifice for the good of others as the great duty of life, could have given a more personal and practical illustration of the tenet than this poor old and uncomely savage. Rough and unpolished as the casket was, it yet held within that priceless gem, a kind heart.

Although the river was high from heavy rains at its source, the season locally had been dry. We were somewhat disappointed with the appearance of the country. In its then uncropped and natural condition, grass was scarce, and the plains were bare, as we found on riding some days' journey up the stream. At one place we surprised a family of natives. We came upon their newly-formed and just-deserted camp. They had seen us and ran away. We saw them streaming like wild animals across the plain. We galloped up to them. They were a man and his wife and young child and two lads. Very frightened and breathless, they jabbered incoherently in an unknown tongue. We gave one of the lads, who looked brave and unconcerned, a shilling, and left them to wonder at the strange animals they had discovered.

Having seen enough of the country, we returned to civilization, having ridden in all some 1200 miles in about eight weeks. Shortly after our return, two of my companions started for the Darling with flocks of sheep and a drove of cattle, and formed stations there. With varying fortunes, the places were held for some eighteen years, and were sold in 1875 at a great profit.

My second trip to the Darling was made in September, 1885, in obedience to a Ministerial invitation to witness the opening of the railway to Bourke.

I " kill two birds with one stone." I see the first railway train reach Bourke, and I meet a mob of cattle from a station in which I have an interest on the Flinders River in Queensland, not far from the Gulf of

Carpentaria. How great the change since 1857. Then the banks of the Darling River were the *ultima Thule* of pastoral occupation. Now the whole country, from the Darling out to the north coast, is taken up and stocked. The railway then was only so far as Parramatta; now it is at Bourke, nearly 500 miles further into the country.

I enter the train at Bathurst, and am at Bourke in about twelve hours. Some part of the way I travel in the Ministerial and Vice-regal car, and am regaled with the choicest delicacies that culinary art can provide. I miss the parrot on damper from the *menu*, however. When we reach Bourke I watch the proceedings from the platform of the car with much amused interest. There is a large pleased crowd there, as indeed there should be on such a great occasion. The old Governor, Lord Loftus, who always looked every inch a Governor in calm dignity and courtesy of manner, receives the congratulatory address of the civic authorities. I notice the town clerk uncovers his head and tucks his soft felt hat under his arm preparatory to commencing the proceedings. The Governor, with true kindness, under that sunny sky, motions him to put on his head cover. He replies, with true Australian independence, " Oh, all right," and braves the chance of sunstroke. Addresses are read and answered, champagne is drunk, and with a " Hip, hip, hip, hurrah!" the party drive round the town in dusty procession. If you complain to a Bourke man of dust, he tells you, " If you want to see dust, you must go to Wilcannia." If you timidly suggest to a Wilcannia man "that the place is rather dusty," he sharply says, " You be d———; you should see Menindie." I have not yet seen a Menindie man. A Wilcannia man will explain to you that even if the dust there is worse than the Bourke dust, and does settle upon you in greater heaps, still, the grains being

I

larger and more sandy, it is more easily brushed off. A scientific and microscopic examination shows the Bourke dust to be composed of more minute, and therefore of more searching, particles than the Wilcannia dust.

At night a great banquet is held in the railway goods shed. The Governor is there, and a Minister of the Crown, and members of Parliament are common enough, and the Mayor of Bourke is in the chair, and there are gorgeous *menu* cards with some symbolic device upon them, and a no less sumptuous dinner brought all the way from Sydney. But I missed that stew of all the birds when we camped by the lagoon, near thirty years ago, and nothing that civilization could offer was a compensation for that joyous independent roughing. And so one of the speakers at the dinner thinks, as he informs his hearers, that "there was a time in Bourke when you could go to sleep securely and leave all your houses open without any fear of molestation, but now, thanks to the railway and the advantages of civilization brought with it, if you leave a window unbolted, and there happens to be a leg of mutton or anything of that sort handy, it is sure to be gone by the morning."

A friend takes me in his buggy to meet the cattle on the opposite side of the river from Bourke. The day is calm and hot, and the roads are dusty. We drive across a large plain, we see a dark spot that dances and quivers in the heated air of noonday. On near approach it proves to be a little girl with a horse. She is alone, and minding some thousands of sheep. She is sitting on the ground in such scanty shade as her horse affords. As we speak, she leaps to her feet like a startled deer and tries to make off, pulling the horse after her. We cannot help noticing how poorly she is clad and how lamentably too short her frayed and torn skirts are to cover her lower limbs. With innate modesty, however, she tries to pull down her dress in order to hide her legs, and not succeeding then tries to double up her legs under the dress. As this succeeds no better, she hides herself behind her horse, and turning her back to us, answers in terrified "Nos" our questions as to the whereabouts of the cattle. We drive off, regretting much to be the unintnetional cause of such distress, my friend exclaiming, " Poor little thing! she is fairly wild; she is fairly wild." We sadden as we think of the dreary life of that poor little lonely child, condemned to follow her sheep in all weathers on that solitary plain.

We find the cattle ; they have travelled 1100 miles— up the Flinders, down the Thompson, across the Barcoo, and *via* the Wilson, Bulloo, Paroo, and Warrego waters—to Bourke. They are still in good condition, and some of them prime fat. But they must be travelled some hundreds of miles further before they are disposed of. They were started from the station on the Flinders in April, they came to Bourke in the first week in September, and were sold at Wodonga, in Victoria, on the last day of November. This will give some idea of one side of squatting operations.

That night at Bourke a grand ball was held, and there were many beautiful cultured ladies there, dressed in the very height of fashion. As I contemplated them I could not help contrasting the three types of womankind my two trips to the Darling have shown me as dwelling on its banks—the poor old savage lubra, with her sharp strong teeth and her kind heart, the solitary little wild white shepherdess on the plains, and the fashionable ladies who have courageously consented to carry a charming civilization and refinement into that unlovely place.

We leave Bourke at midnight. As the train glides

12

slowly past the building where the ball is held, the band plays a beautiful melody. We hear the sweet music with clear sharpness in the cool night air. That and the rhythmic cadence of the dancers' feet, heard in measured time, leave a last and pleasing impression of the place, too soon lost as we rush away into the dark.

LOST CHILDREN.

JIM MAYBUD and his wife and small family lived in an isolated hut built on the banks of a lagoon, in one of those watercourses (almost peculiar to Australia) which " hardly ever " contain running streams. This creek is in the flat country between two of the large rivers. Except in unusually wet seasons its waters never find their way into the main channel, but are exhausted in filling long and deep sinuous lagoons, which are joined or threaded together by a broad, shallow, tree and grass overgrown channel, so indistinct in places that one might ride across it without suspecting its character. On the banks of the lagoons grow large blue-gum trees, a sure indication, if not of permanent, at least of water sufficiently lasting to encourage pastoral settlement. The country around is almost level, and is covered by forests and patches of various species of trees, each kind apparently choosing or being chosen by soils of differing characters, and seldom encroaching on each other's domain. On the red loamy ground the white box thickly, interspersed with cypress and with rather dense undergrowth of acacia, predominates. On the low-lying, black, flooded land, the belar, a species of native oak or casuarina, is found, casting so dense a shade as to prevent all other vegetation from showing. When these thickets are killed by ring-barking, the long-fallowed soil produces exceptionally luxuriant grass and herbage. There are occasionally large park-like areas of the pretty pendulous light-grey myall, which tree appears to float cloudlike when shown in strong relief against the dark branches of the belar. In these patches there grows profusely a sickly-looking greenish-yellow shrub, locally misnamed the currant bush. Its fruit is a pea. The best and most fattening grasses grow among the myalls. The yarran, an acacia, like the myall having violet-scented wood, is widely dispersed, and frequently fringes the myall patches with its olive-green foliage. The prickly hakea and the native-named "warriah bush," almost leafless with its small purple berries, grow everywhere. This country is used as a cattle run, and has not long been occupied. The lands are unenclosed, the fencing stage of civilization not having as yet developed itself.

Jim Maybud is the stockman in charge of the place, and is breaking in a small herd to the run. His duty is to ride out every day and find all or the most of his cattle, and satisfy himself that they keep within bounds. If he misses any he must look for their tracks, and follow them up till found. Sometimes, in spite of his care, mobs will stray away and become mixed with far off herds, and then he has to start off on horseback, with blanket and quart-pot and hob-bles, to attend musters at these places and bring back the truants. It was a very happy-go-lucky and

improvident style of management, which, however, the
general system of fencing adopted later put a stop
to. Jim's hut has four rooms; the walls are of split
pine slabs, the joints, or rather disjoints, are filled with
a mortar of cowdung and loam, and inside and out
the walls are whitewashed with a kind of pipeclay
found on the banks of the main river many miles away.
Jim's wife must have some whitewash, so when the
cattle have " settled down a bit," quite an expedition
is made, occupying some days, in order to procure that
which, when applied, does brighten up the appearance
of things a little.   Of the two front rooms, shaded by
a narrow verandah, Jim and his wife and the youngest
child occupy one, the other is used as a kitchen and
eating room ; of the skillions, one is a store for the
rations, and the other is the older children's room.
A few yards in front of the hut is the saddle-
pole, a long pine log resting in box forks. When the
day's work is done, the saddles and horse gear are
placed astride this pole. Under the verandah, in a
cage made of an old tea-chest, is one of the pretty little
cockatoo parrots. Most engaging little creatures they
are, and can be taught to say anything. It is a great
pet, the children are very fond of it, and it is very fond
of the children, that is if the fact that whenever it sees
them it dances up and down its perch, puts its head
through the bars of the cage and says, with anxious repetition, " kiss pretty Joey," is any evidence of it.
    A couple of dogs are generally lying asleep near the
saddle pole, and when an occasional neighbour rides up
they rush out and bark furiously.   When the man dismounts and ties up his horse at the pole they suddenly
seem to know that they have done wrong, and look out
into the bush and make believe they are barking at
something else they see out there, then they scrape their
hind feet vigourously on the ground, and growl and

snap at each other, and seize each other by the throat, and roll over each other in the dust, all which is by way apology to the guest for the uncivil, surly greeting, and he is meant to understand that each thinks the other to be " a most confounded fool" for such conduct. Then they come to him wagging their tails, and fawn upon him and lick his hands, and snuff at his heels, till he enters the door, when they stretch themselves and yawn, and go back to their lairs and fall asleep again, having first given a flea (behind an ear) "fits" with their hinder claws. This process has just been gone through as a neighbour arrives from the nearest station about three miles off. He is known as Bathurst Tom. His residence is a duplicate of Jim's. He is married, and has an only child—a nice little, bright-eyed daughter, Polly—about eleven years of age. Polly often finds her way through the bush to play with the little Maybuds. Tom is a tall, slim, active fellow, who moves as gracefully as a greyhound. He has broad upright shoulders, although his limbs are somewhat long and lanky. His forehead is oblong, and squarer and broader than high, denoting considerable force and manliness of character. His eyes are blue and frank, and turn from no one's gaze. From his chin depends a magnificent yellow beard. No buckjumper ever foaled could throw Tom. His hollow thighs and evenly-balanced body enabled him to stick like "grim death" to the pigskin. Tom by-and-by will become the manager and the partner of a great city capitalist in pastoral properties, and grow wealthy and a notable man in the district. He is greeted at the door by his hostess, who comes out wiping her hands with her apron. She is always busy cleaning up something, and everything in that hut is as clean as a new pin. The Queen herself might eat her meals in that hut without having her fastidious delicacy offended. Mrs. Maybud is very famous for her " pufftalooners." These are a kind of small cake made of yeast sponge, and are fried in fresh fat or butter, and when properly made and cooked with a crisp brown crust upon them, and served with fresh nutty kangaroo grass butter and new-laid eggs boiled just three minutes and a half (not a grain of sand more or less), make a meal fit for an emperor, not even excepting Heliogabalus from the number.

The good wife is of about twenty-five years, the most charming of all matronly ages. No puny weakling, but full 5ft. 6in. in height, straight, active, and rounded—no great beauty, perhaps, as measured by city standards : her chaste grey eyes ; her white teeth showing not too prominently under slightly parted pink, full lips ; her glossy, smooth, brown hair, always neat and tidy, in massive braids

————" bespread,
" **Madonna-wise, on either side her head;**"

her slightly sun-browned complexion, and her fresh healthy look, make her a very pleasant object to contemplate. She is always good humoured and friendly and hospitable, and when one takes his leave of her he is sensible that the hand shake is too formal, and he experiences an almost irresistible impulse to take her in his arms and kiss her. She is so bright and bonny, and so sweet and pure, one feels that the more heart-felt expression is more fully her due, and the only proper way to part from so much womanly goodness. But alas! there are Jim and the proprieties, and Jim, backed up by the proprieties, is rather a formidable obstacle to this sweet familiarity. So you must content yourself with the common formality, and not let her know how much you envy Jim the possession of his treasure. The wonder is how Jim, who is rather a dull but honest fellow, managed to draw such a prize in the matrimonial lottery. When you contemplate the pair, you find your-self involuntarily repeating after Philip van Artevelde—

> ————" Outward grace
> Nor outward light is needful ; day by day
> Men wanting both are mated with the best
> And loftiest of God's feminine creation,
> Whose love takes no distinction but of gender,
> And ridicules the very name of choice."

What a consolation is the philosophical burgher's reflection to those unsuccessful men who fail to win fair lady !

Although Tom is a married man and loves his wife, he cannot help looking with softened gentle approval upon the trim figure and kind service of his hostess.

I remember when once in search of new country, and over a hundred miles from any human residence, and after a long weary ride through profitless mallee and spinifex desert, coming suddenly upon a small open plain, covered with luxuriant grass. In its very centre grew a beautiful clianthus plant in full bloom, it coloured, beautified, and enriched the whole scene. So like this desert flower Mary Maybud, with her gentle, modest, cheerful womanhood shed a refining influence on all who in that remote place came within its range. Even Dick the Devil's foul, blasphemous tongue was silenced in the presence of her sweet purity ; and if any man among the rough ones who occasionally came to muster at the station had dared indecency within earshot of her, he would have been then and there kicked and sent to Coventry.

Tom has ridden over to learn from his neighbour if he has seen any of his stray cattle. James is not at home, so Tom will stay while Mrs. Maybud prepares some pufftalooners and eggs and tea. While the meal is preparing the children climb up on his knees. One in particular, Little Jim, four years old, buries his hands

in the yellow beard, and prattles about Polly. Now
Polly is Jim's great chum. She has no brothers or
sisters of her own, so her affectionate little heart and
instincts all flow out towards Jim. He is a fine sturdy,
robust little chap, with curly hair and round red cheeks,
and a manly air about him very taking to Tom, who,
when the meal is ready, sets him down with a sigh,
wishing his little Polly had just such another one for a
brother. As Jim's feet touch the floor, he says, slowly
and thoughtfully, " I'se goin' a see Polly."

Tom has lately come from the nearest village and
post-town, nigh a hundred miles away, and has picked
up some of the news of the great outside world, and has
a story to tell of the fall of Sebastopol, and the end of
the Crimean war (for 'tis over thirty years since) and
they chat and gossip about numberless other things : of
the doings of the sparsely scattered neighbours ; of
births and marriages, most pleasant sounds to female
ears ; of stations on the river changing hands, for the
discovery of gold, like a magician's wand, has worked
wonderful transformations here. Men who thought
themselves poor, suddenly, as at the brushing of
Aladdin's lamp, became " rich beyond the dreams of
avarice," such " potentialities " were there in grass and
water turned into beef and mutton and wool. So
speculation was rife, and much buying and selling is
going on. Tom is clever and talkative in his way, and
his hostess, not having seen a soul for weeks but her
own belongings, finds his pleasant gossip brightens solitude, and makes life less dreary to her. So the hours
pass away unheeded, and near sundown the husband
comes home, and the two friends talk over their business. When the evening meal is ready, the children,
whose merry prattle has always been within hearing
distance, are called in, and the mother says, " Where is
little Jim ?" The little things stare blankly, and say

they "don't know." The mother, not then anxious, goes out and calls Jim, and peers into all likely places. But Jim neither answers nor is seen. She comes back to her husband, and with a slight tremor in her voice, born of fears she does not like to admit, says, "I cannot find Jim! where can he be?" "Oh, he is all right!" says the father, "he can't be far away." Noticing his wife's incipient alarm, and anxious to please her, he goes out and calls and cooeys and looks into all possible and impossible places, and at length, as night closes in, the reality forces itself upon them. Poor little Jim must be lost! and, good God! where? The two men snatch a hasty cup of tea, and catch their horses and ride about separately, not far from the hut, for Jim cannot be long gone. They call his name softly. They do not cooey, for that might be a deceptive signal to each other, if he is not found. After an hour or so is passed they return to the hut, but the mother has not discovered him, so they at once start off again to make wider search, and not return till daylight. All this time the anxious mother, with a sinking feeling about her heart, goes in and out, peering into the dark and listening. There is nothing to be seen but the stars above and the great gaunt trees with their impenetrable shade, and nothing to be heard but the beating of her own heart, the weird cry of some night bird, and the melancholy sighing of the night wind through the oaks. She has no desire for rest, and is filled with a painful wakefulness that cannot be allayed. Sleep would be so criminal, with her darling little boy astray.

Near morning she hears the horsemen returning. She runs out to meet them. Jim dismounts as his wife draws near. Tom, with true courtesy, turns off and rides another way. Mary puts a hand upon each of her husband's shoulders, and with tearful eyes, looking him in the face, says, "Oh, Jim! you have never come back without him." Jim looks askance at the lagoon; the action adds force to the fearful suspicion growing within her. "Oh, not there Jim, not there!" she exclaims, as she buries her head in her husband's bosom and gives way and weeps as though her heart would break. All that Jim, poor dull clod, can do is to stroke her beautiful hair with his great rough hand, and say tremulously, "Poor old woman, poor old woman." This burst of grief over, they return to the hut, where Tom is already come. They have been riding all night, so Mary's kindly instinct busies itself in getting refreshment for them, and they discuss more calmly the plans of search for the day. The horses too must be cared for, so Tom hobbles them and turns them into a bend of the lagoon where the best grass is. As soon as it is light they search along the edge of the lagoon. The water in it has been receding, and leaves a narrow band of wet mud between its surface and the drier part of the bank. A tomtit could not walk into the water without leaving a visible track there. This muddy band is examined, and no sign of little Jim's footsteps is seen anywhere, so they are quite sure he is not in the water.

They now decide to seek more assistance. While the father remains to continue the search Tom goes home to tell his wife of the unhappy accident, and then rides to the river to S——'s station to see if some blacks and a party can be got together to make a surer and more systematic search. Tom reaches the station late in the day. There is a number of men there, as a muster is going on. He is well known, and after friendly greetings tells the story, states his mission, and asks for volunteers. The first to speak is Dick the Devil. Dick has acquired his satanic nickname partly because of his mad fearlessness. He has been known to run in a great wild stallion, a descendant of unbroken sires and dams for generations past, to rope him, put saddle and bridle on him, mount him there and then, and stick to him and conquer him. He has been known, from a pure spirit of daring fun, to drop from a stock-yard gate on the back of a wild bullock as he ran through, and come to no harm therefrom. He chiefly earned his name from his limited vocabulary, which was composed of few words save oaths, obscenity, and blasphemous profanity. Strange to say, these words were almost perfectly innocent in Dick's idea. He knew but few others. So rugged was his speech that I doubt if this chaste page would dare to tell of Dick's morning salutation to a friend. I once camped out with a party of which Dick formed one. The atmo-sphere surrounding Dick's dialogue was simply a lurid horror. No one knew who he was or whence he came. He was a newcomer in the district. He departed mys-teriously, no one knew where. In the minds of some he was thought to be identified with a bushranger who a long time after died the death of a dog from a trooper's revolver, but the truth was never known. However, to Dick's credit, he was the first to volunteer for this busi-ness, and offered to bring his black assistant. As another man or two and black also offered to go, Tom's party is complete. They start off at once, and reaching Jim's hut a few hours before daybreak, they learn from him of his unsuccessful search again. They hobble their horses and lie down to snatch some little rest. Mary's hospitable care (completely worn out, she had slept a little during the night,) preparing breakfast for them before the stars were off the sky roused up the men. When there is light enough the blacks are set to work. Using the lagoon as a base, they start from dif-ferent points, so as to enclose the hut (the last place the boy was seen) in a semicircle. In a short time one gives a cooey. The other immediately goes to him.

They look closely on the ground; they consult together, and decide that they have found the track. If you and I, dear reader, were to take a magnifying glass, and go down upon our knees and examine what they see, we would make nothing of it. Long ages of natural selection and heredity have given them this wonderful power. Their brains are mostly in their eyes. They are sure, and one comes and tells what they have seen while the other follows on the tracks, walking slowly, with head bent towards the ground. He goes neither to the right nor left, but with wonderful patience and keen sightedness looks for and finds signs of each footstep. At news of this discovery, the mother's heart grows lighter and almost cheerful as the black says to her, " Nebber you mind now, missis; we'll find him that one now, baal gammon." So the men saddle their horses and take their blankets and some provisions, not forgetting a bottle of milk to restore little Jim when he is found. They will not return now (thanks to the blacks) till he is found, as every step must bring them nearer to him. The anxious mother watches them as they disappear in the forest, following with 'her eyes that bent figure marching slowly on, looking ever on the ground. The two blacks take turn and turn about. They never lose the trail. Sometimes they have to cast back a few yards, but they are never long at fault.

The whites as they go scour the scrubby country on each side with praiseworthy impatience, but nothing comes of it. At one place the blacks come to a dead myall lying on the ground, with spiked ends of its branches sticking out. They minutely examine one of the spikes. "You see it that one," says one, pointing to a sharp spike. " Little Jimmy been scratch him face along a that one," putting his finger on his cheek to indicate the spot. As they proceed, they find where the little fellow has drunk water from the " gilgais " or shallow pools, has pulled wild flowers, has eaten the berries from the "warriah" bushes, has lain down overcome, and has slept and roused himself and travelled on again. At length night overtakes them, and they camp near a large gilgai in a myall forest, where his footsteps in the mud as he lapped the water are very plain and fresh. They hunt round in the dark, but to no purpose, and they lie down and wait for the morning.

The mother endures another lonely, wakeful night. She feels that every hour as it now passes by makes hope of finding her boy alive less certain. But when, her children kneeling on the bed with uplifted hands clasped in hers and pressed to her bosom, she teaches them to say "Pray God bless and keep little Jim," she feels that the simple petition of her sinless little ones has a practical significance never known before. It is not a mere formality and vain repetition now, and heavenly hope lightens the grief at her heart as she believes that the prayer may be heard. But with that peculiar process of the mind that in distress, how hopeful soever it may be, anticipates the worst, and exercises itself in providing for all contingencies, she cannot drive away from her the thought that her boy's dead body may be brought to her, and if so, what shall be done ?

Near the hut is a large wilgar tree, the most shapely and beautiful of all trees in that region. Under this tree, in its dense shade, it has been her practice to sit sewing while her children played around her. She now begins to associate with this tree a little grave, as a future possibility. During the night, as often as she goes to the door to listen, her glance will, with a fearsome fascination, turn towards the tree, and in imagination picture to herself a little mound of piled-up earth, under which her child will lie. It is only by a strong exercise of the will that she prevents herself from

going there to choose the spot. Sometimes, in spite of
herself, she dozes and falls asleep and wakes with a
start and blames herself that she can be so careless:
and so another dreary night goes on. Early next
morning Tom's wife and Polly come to her. When the
women meet, they fall upon each others' neck and
weep; and little Polly, too, is very tearful as she misses
her little playfellow. But it is a great comfort to the
mother to have them with her, and she becomes
calmer, and with much mental reproach almost forgets
her grief.

Next day, and apparently at a mile or two from where
the men are camped, a bellowing of cattle is heard, of
that peculiar sound which cannot be described, but is
given out by them when anything unusual attracts
their notice. One of the blacks says sharply, " You
hear him that one, that fellow find him little boy. Baal
gammon ! Jim sit down there where that one cattle
make it that one row. That one ' gindie ' (play around)
along a little Jimmie. We find him now, my word !
budgeree that one ! baal gammon ! ! " So they run to
their horses, which have been tied up for better security
during the greater part of the night, and saddle and
mount in hot haste, and start off at a gallop for the
place of the noise, for the cattle still " gindie " about
something. Soon they see the backs of the cattle over
the low currant bushes under the myalls, and the pace
increases; but by general consent of the rest, Jim's
father is allowed to take the lead. None would be so
ungenerous as to rob him of the pleasure of being the
first to find his boy. So in this order they reach the
spot, and there sure enough is little Jim. The cattle
are are so intent upon him, bellowing around him, that
at first they do not notice the horsemen, who see Jim
standing manfully with his face to the foe. And then the
cattle scamper off, and the boy sees the horsemen, and

thinks he has new foes to face, and stands bravely, with
one foot advanced, his two little hands tight clenched
on bunches of wild flowers. His father jumps off his
horse and takes up his boy in his arms, and sobs over
him, and the rest take off their hats and shout " Hip,
hip, hoorah !" and look at each other, and laugh with a
laugh as nearly hysterical as a man can go ; and they
all get off and take up Jim, and hold him out at arms'
length and say, " Hullo, Jim! how are you, Jim, old
fellow ?" Little Jim, pale and tired, makes but one
reply, very touching to Tom, who wipes his eye with the
back of his hand as the boy gasps out slowly to each
as they hold him out, " Ise a goin' a see Polly. I
wants a give her dese flowers." And the blacks
speak to him, and say, " Well, Jimmy, what you
think a long a blackfellow now, eh ?" And their eyes
glisten with pleasure as they show their white teeth,
and the scratch is seen on the child's face just where
the blacks said it would be found. The boy does not
understand the meaning of all this. In childlike fancy
he is still lured on by the kind sympathetic face of
Polly, whose place he is quite sure is only "just over
there." They carry him back to the night's camp, and
make a bed for him with all the blankets, and they
warm the milk and make a sop for him, after which he
is much better. Then they pack up and start for home,
some miles away, carrying Jim by turns, and he dozes
in their arms as they ride along. When he is changed
from one to the other he half awakes, and sleepily tries to
say, " Ise goin' a see Polly." As they near home, the poor
mother, hearing afar off the noise of the horses' feet,
runs out to meet them, not knowing what to hope or
what to fear. With instinctive courtesy, the father and
boy are allowed to go first and far in advance, and the
mother takes her boy in her arms and, nearly smothering him with kisses, cries over him in the excess of her

K

gladness, and is half inclined to scold him for all the trouble he has given, but she refrains. So all is joy and brightness again in the little household. After they break their fast the men must all part, for they have other business on hand. Before they go, Jim, the father, tries to make a little speech to them, but woefully breaks down and fails, for Jim is not much given to sentiment. Unfortunately, in Jim's school sentiment has always been laughed to scorn as worthy only of a regular milksop. All Jim can do is to give each a warm grasp of the hand and say, " Thank you, boys ; I'll do as much for you some time," which offer of help they hope they will never need.

When they say good-by to the mother she takes the great rough hands of each in her soft palms, and with tears of gladness welling in her honest eyes, looks him in the face and utters a grateful mother's gracious heartfelt thanks, and she feels as if she would like to put her arms round their necks and kiss them all (not even excepting Dick the Devil) in the fullness of her gratitude. But then there are Jim and the proprieties. And so those rough young fellows ride away, feeling in their hearts, although they would think it unmanly to admit so much to each other, that they are none the worse, but all the better, for having been engaged in that charitable act, thinking, too, that it is no small privilege to be enshrined in the memory of so sweet and pure-minded a woman; that is, if they were able to think so much, which, at least, is doubtful. And now little Polly has her turn, and she takes up Jim on her lap. She sits on a lowly stool and lavishes childish endearments upon him as he gives her the wild flowers (all crushed and withered) he has never ceased to hold. She pretends to be angry for his roving, at which new experience Jim opens his round eyes very wide, but kissing away an incipient whimper, she makes him promise he will " not never no more go off into the bush again by himself," because she will always come to him when he wants her.

Another mother was not so fortunate as Mary Maybud. She was a bright, warm-hearted Irish girl, homely and plain all to her eyes, which were the finest ever seen in a woman. They were large, full, light hazel-coloured orbs, glistening with merriment and genial fun. When her clear silvery laugh followed the merry flash of her eyes, the mirthful contagion was irresistible.

She had a little boy, named Patsy, with his mother's eyes, but showing a strange difference. There was a spiritual melancholy in their depths when he looked at you in that trustful, wistful way, more often seen in the eyes of some dumb animal than in a human being, that made him very interesting to look upon. This was afterwards remembered as showing evidence of some premonition of his sad fate.

He was a solitary little fellow, and much preferred to be alone than have playfellows. The day he was missed, when night came it was certain he was lost. The country around was hilly and stony and thickly timbered. There were large, deep holes full of water in the creek that ran close by. The services of blacks were secured, but, by a fatal mistake, the use made of them was to dive to its depths and search the water.

He was not found there, and valuable time was lost, as the tracks of the station sheep driven in and out to grass destroyed all chance of finding the signs of his footsteps. Other search was made, but Patsy was not then found. The poor mother's character altered from that day. She was ever after subdued by a settled sadness. All desire to laugh or to create laughter in others had completely died within her. Her eyes grew like to her little boy's eyes, and lost all their light and merriment.   Another boy was shortly after born to her, whom she also called Patsy. This Patsy in his mother's mind had no individuality of his own.   He was looked upon by her as merely a representative of the little one she had lost.   All caresses lavished on him were given in memory of his lost brother.   She was a strict Roman Catholic.   The thought that her boy's remains did not lay in consecrated ground haunted her like a nightmare. Many months after, a lad who was shepherding sheep, having followed them away out to the top of a dreary outlying high mountain, towering over a deep valley called the Devil's Hole, and miles away from the station, noticed the leading sheep of the flock to start and turn back.   Curiosity excited, he went to see what was there.   Amid a heap of rocks, over which, worn and weak, he had staggered and stumbled and fallen to rise no more, lay the bones of poor little Patsy.   They were identified by some small piece of metal adornment and a rotting remnant of a many-coloured raiment which his mother recognised as having been worn by him when he strayed.   The remains were gathered together and received burial.   All uncertainty now at an end, the poor mother regained some of her elasticity of spirit, and she learned to love her second Patsy for himself alone ; for

> " Pain and grief
> Are transitory things, no less than joy ;
> And though they leave us not the men we were,
> Yet they do leave us."

IN DREAMLAND.

> " There are more things in heaven and earth, Horatio,
> Than are dreamt of in our philosophy."

I HAVE been told the following dreams from most credible sources. They are, if not remarkable, at least curious. I will not attempt explanation of them, although I am firmly convinced that they may be fully accounted for on purely natural grounds, and may be traced to suggestions of wakeful thoughts and ideas, without falling back upon the supernatural and poetical vagueness of the above quotation to find reasons for them :—

I.—PAT BOURKE'S GRANDCHILD.

Pat Bourke was an Irishman of the best type of his class. He emigrated with his family in the "forties," in Governor Gipps's time, when we had such a large accession of population from that source. In the old days, before the diggings, he and his family had charge of two flocks of sheep. His wage for self, wife and son was £55 per annum, with rations—that is to say, he and his son had £20 each as shepherds, and his wife £15 as hutkeeper, and very happy and contented were they. He was a large, robust, well-made man, full of good humour and geniality. Honest and straightforward, his employer's interest was his sole matter of concernment. Very like in personal appearance to Tenniel's John Bull in *Punch*, he was altogether without any sentimentalism whatever, and at the same time intelligently superior to most of his order. He had a daughter, Mary, married to a shepherd in the same service. The hut where Mary and her husband lived was a few miles away, on the brow of a low hill. At the foot of the hill was a watercourse, having a broad grass overgrown bed, in which were occasional deep round ponds. In the front of the hut, and on the slope towards the creek, were the sheepyards—enclosures with high paling fences,—and just beyond them was one of the deep round ponds. One morning Pat woke up, and told his wife that he'd had "a very quare dhrame." He dreamed that Mary's boy, a little chap just able to run about, was drowned in the hole at the back of the yards. The whole thing was shown so plainly to him, that, with all his common sense, he could not argue himself out of the idea but that something evil had happened. So he determined to send his little daughter Peggy over to Mary's and make quite sure that there was no truth in his dream. Peggy, nothing loth, wishing to have a chat with her sister and see her little nephew, started off on her solitary walk through the bush. This place is on the high tableland, between the Turon and Cudgegong rivers, and was seldom, if ever, visited by any except those belonging to the station. A few years after, and tens of thousands of human beings were wandering about through its hills and valleys in search of hidden treasures. Our little maiden of fourteen years, as her path led her up a long gully, over a low ridge, and down another long gully shaded by high white gums, walked over fortunes all unknown to her. It was in the early summer time. The land was bright with flowers. The Kennedyas hung in purple masses from the bushes over which they had trained themselves. The buttercups on the low ground, making fields of " cloth of gold " in yellow brilliance,

were prophetic of the mineral wealth that lay in undis-
turbed repose about their roots. "Cherry-pie" *(pime-
lia)* and native primroses and the yellow lilies shed their
fragrance in the air. Not a cloud was to be seen in the
bright blue sky; not a breath of air rustled the metallic
leaves of the trees, as from their great height and lofty
dignity they seemed, to her at least, with their arms
spread over her, to look down and contemplate the little
maiden with a pleasant regard as she tripped along.
They appeared to rest in a hushed silence until she
passed out of sight, when probably they nodded to each
other and murmured in gentle approval. The stillness
of the forest was broken by the note of the solitary
banbandarlo, whistled in soft, melancholy sweetness,
and from which it has its native name. Numbers of
swiftly flying paraquets, screeching shrilly, darted like
living emeralds with green glitter through the topmost
branches of the honey-scented flowering gums, or hung
like pendant jewels from the great clusters of snowy
blossoms from which they sucked the juices, chirping
not unmusically the while. A great iguana would now
and again scuttle in shambling awkwardness across the
path and scramble up the nearest tree, from behind the
stem of which, as it stealthily crawled up, it would look
askance at little Peggy, like some impish demon peering
and mocking at her, but prevented by fate or fear from
approaching within the charmed circle of defence which
her innocence and virgin purity formed around her; all
the same, their presence made her feel not a little
"skeery" and horror-haunted. "Old-men kangaroos"
as they heard her step would leap from the ground and
bound a few paces and turn back and look at her, prop-
ping themselves up with their tails, their paws hanging
at their sides like hands; and as she came nearer would
again bound away, and then turn and look with their
great liquid eyes again, and at length, feeling them-

selves to be at a safe distance, hop away slowly out of
sight. Altogether it was one of those delicious days
midway between winter and summer that makes existence itself a real pleasure. Peggy had frequently
travelled this lonely track, and as often as she had gone
had with true female tenderness and love for them
gathered bunches of wild flowers for her sister's little
boy. Now she involuntarily culled some as she went
along, but as the thought of the dream and its not im-
probable truth flashed across her mind, she dropped
them with a sigh, and hurried on, blaming herself for
loitering on such important business. She was not
sorry when at length the solitude of her walk was
broken by the sight of her sister's dwelling, and the
feeling quickened to intense delight, as the first living
object she saw was the little boy playing about in joyful
glee near the door. As she neared the place she passed
quite close to the dreaded pond with its dense fringe of
high green rushes and its tawny-coloured water, stained
by the bark and leaves shed from the adjacent trees,
and looking as it reflected the sun's rays like a piece of
polished bronze set in bright green velvet edging. It
was so unruffled and peaceful, and looked so unhurtful,
that Peggy, with ease now at her heart, could scarcely
refrain from laughing outright as she bounded up the
hill and caught her little nephew in her arms, and half-
smothering him with kisses, carried him into the hut.
Then sitting on a stool (with the boy standing up on
her lap, his arms around her neck, and his warm little
cheek pressed fondly against hers) almost breathless
and half-ashamed, she tells her sister the cause of her
visit. They laugh at the grandfather's groundless
alarm, and the mother, taking the boy in her arms and
pressing him to her bosom, declares that there is "no
fear of Johnny being drowned; they take too much
care of him for that." And now Peggy, having rested,

will have a cup of tea and some more solid refreshment, and must then hurry off to tell her father not to dream any more such silly things with needless frightenings. So the boy is set down and he goes outside, and they hear him running after the fowls, which will always come about the door when they know that meals are going on inside. Peggy chats with her sister about family and sheep station news, and about all the trouble she has had with various refractory old ewes at the lambing time who would not look at nor suckle their own lambs, "unnatural old things that they were." And she puts on her hood, and her sister kisses her and says "good-by," and gives another kiss for the father and mother. And now where is little Johnny to say good-by to and kiss? They go outside expecting to find him near the door; but he is not there. They call him, but he does not answer; and in an agony, pale and breathless, they rush down as by an instinctive impulse to the pond, and there is his hat floating on the water and his little body drowned—dead—and lying too still just under its surface. The disturbed rippling water seems to wink and blink in the sunlight with an expression of malicious satisfaction at the mischief it has done. And so poor sorrowing little Peggy has to retrace her solitary path with the sad story that somehow her father's dream has brought about its own fulfilment.

II.—THE MASTER AND THE MAN.

Application had been made to the Government for another man-servant to be assigned. When a new batch arrived at the nearest settlement and barracks, one was sent out to the farm in charge of a constable. As he was quite new to colonial ways, he was kept there for some time, so as to obtain a little bush experience. He was then despatched to a sheep-station

—strange to say, the very one where the little boy was drowned.   He had some thirty miles to walk by himself through the bush, across the Turon River, and up over the high ranges on the farther side, and was then directed to find certain marked trees, and to go from tree to tree, then to follow certain watercourses, then more marked trees and more watercourses, and that would bring him to the shepherd's hut.   If he lost his marks, he was to follow down the first watercourse he came to and not leave it, and that would be sure to lead him to some habitation.   With confident ignorance he started off, ridiculing the idea of ever becoming lost. He found his way to the Turon, about half his journey, but from that place he never could tell where he went.   A few days after his master learned that he did not reach his destination.   What was become of him ? Had he absconded or was he lost ?   The last supposition was relied upon, and all available hands turned out to search for him.   Nothing was seen of him that day, and at night his master, very anxious for his discovery, dreamt that the man had arrived at the station, that at night the shepherds' dogs had suddenly rushed out barking at something, that the shepherds went out to see what it was, and they found the lost man, almost completely exhausted, crawling on his hands and knees through a brokendown part of an old boughyard, and making towards the light in the hut.   Such was the dream, and so convinced was the dreamer of the truth of the vision that he ordered the search to be discontinued, and dispatched a special messenger to the place, who came back with the news that the man had been found exactly in the manner seen in the dream.

III.—The Publican and the Robbers.

Alick L——— and his wife had for a long time been servants to a squatter on the Lachlan.   Alick, in the capacity of stockman, had managed somehow or another (we will not inquire too closely into the method) to acquire a considerable sum of money, or rather he had managed to get together a number of cattle and horses, which he sold for a considerable sum of money. He did not retire upon his fortune, but opened a public-house on the river bank. It was rather a quiet, out-of-the-way place until the Forbes diggings "broke out," when a good deal of traffic passing his door, he was supposed to be making a lot of money. The household consisted of his wife—a very pretty young woman—their children, and a man named Ned Smith. One day Alick and his friend Smith started off on business to Forbes, some twelve miles away. When they were about half a mile from home, crossing a deep creek, they saw some men camped. One of these came to them and asked for direcctions about the road. The publican and his friend went on their way for a short time, when the first suddenly pulled rein and said, " By Jove, Ned, we must go back ; that fellow with the beard is the very man I dreamt about the other night, and that came to stick up the place." They rode back, and when they came to the creek they found the men were gone, so they pushed on rapidly to the house. As soon as they came close they were fired at by a man in the verandah, who luckily, or rather unluckily perhaps for Alick, in view of subsequent events, missed Ned, who gallopped off towards a neighbour's station to give the alarm. The robbers, too, having been thus unexpectedly surprised, made off. The good wife, for reasons of her own, had put all the money in the house, in a small bag. Seeing the men approach with arms in their hands, she threw the bag into a large hole thickly overgrown with herbage, and so the robbers were baulked of a prize. The strange part of the story is that, although Alick was warned of these robbers in a dream, his waking thoughts were unable to discover a more successful thief in his friend Ned, who thought it better that no risks of a similar kind should be run in the future, and shortly after eloped with the wife, and they took with them all the money she had so cleverly concealed.

IV.—THE YOUNG GIRL AND THE OLD STOCKMAN.

Mary McM—— was a " currency lass " of about six-teen years, very healthy and wholesome and pleasant to look upon. Very useful, too, to her mother at the cattle station where they were employed. With jet black hair and large dark-blue eyes, and rich brunette complexion, so seldom seen except among those of Milesian parent-age, Mary, when engaged, as she often was, in such occupation, was an Australian representative of the girl of the Irish song—

" Ma colleen dhas cruithen a mo."

And very picturesque or statuesque she looked, too, as she walked along with a vessel full of milk poised upon her head, her tall, slight figure all the more erect and upright from the exertion required to carry the load. One morning, as Mary was helping her mother with the simple household duties, she was noticed by her to be unusually silent and preoccupied. " What's the matter with ye, Mary," said the mother, " are ye in love, my dear ?" " Faith then, I'm not, mother. Last night I had such a fearful dream, and I cannot get rid of it. I thought I saw poor old Sweepy killed. He was not riding his piebald pony, but a black horse with a short tail, and he was run against a tree and killed on the spot." And the girl gave a shudder as she told it. " I should not wonder if that is his fate some day," said the mother, " for the old fellow has taken to drink a good deal lately, and he's a regular harum-scarum on a horse." "Sweepy," as aforesaid, a stockman for the same establishment, was an "old hand." He had earned this name from the fact of his having been in his boyhood a chimney-sweeper's apprentice. He was not now young, and was a wizened, wiry, smoke-dried-looking little creature, with a most unresting energy. Nothing in the shape of wild horses or cattle could escape from Sweepy's untiring pursuit when mounted on his piebald pony Bonaparte. He had all the sharp wit of a London arab, and all the mendacity of his early training. He would rather tell a lie than tell the truth. He was of Bacon's opinion that "a mixture of a lie doth even add pleasure." Any fool could tell the truth; but there was no fun in that ; making fools of people by telling lies did add some flavour to life. At least that's something like what Sweepy's mental process was when he thought about truth. There was only one person he was truthful to, and that was his master. At the same time he would "lie as fast as a horse could gallop" if he thought he could serve his master by so doing. There was really no necessity for it, but still he pre-ferred it. Sometimes his master, by way of joke, would practice upon this habit of his, and call him to bear witness before strangers as to the truth of some pur-posely-invented story. Sweepy on such occasions was never taken aback. He would with all possible gravity assert that what his master said was perfectly true, and make extravagant additions to the tale. Shortly after Mary told her dream to her mother, who should appear unexpectedly but Sweepy and a friend, and he was riding not his pony, but a black short-tailed horse. As soon as he dismounted, after he had chaffed Mary, and pretended to make love to her, she told her dream. "I always like pretty girls like you to dream about me, only the dreams always go by contraries, you know," said he, as he ran after the girl to catch and kiss her in a fatherly sort of way. " Like old Mick Murray's dream—did you hear of that ? No? Well, then, old Mick, the ration carrier, the other day at the farm, goes to the missus, and he says: ' I dhreamt a quare dhrame last night.' 'What was it, Mick?' says she. ' Why, I dhreamt, ma'am, that you gave me half a pound of tebaccy out of the store, and the masther gave me a bran new pair of boots.' 'Ah,' says she, ' but dreams always go by contraries.' ' Is that so ?' says Mick, scratching his head ; ' faith, thin, I believe you're right, ma'am, and maybe it will be the masther that will give me the baccy, and it's yourself that'll give me the boots.' Well, the missus could not help laughing at Mick's dream, and she gave him both the boots and the baccy." " Well," said Mary, laughing, " I only hope my dream won't come as near true as Mick's." Sweepy and his friend ride away, and in an hour or so the friend comes gallopping back to say he lay dead on the road, killed by being run against a tree. It would appear that they had a bottle of rum with them, and having partaken too freely, a race on a level piece of road was proposed, which ended with this fatal result. " I could have better spared a better man," said his master, when he heard of it.

ROUGH SKETCHES IN BLACK AND WHITE.

I.—How Tim Flaherty Won Peace with Honour.

IN the good or bad old days (whichever you like), when Governor Gipps held sway, there stepped on shore, from an emigrant ship, in Sydney Cove, my old friend Tim Flaherty. His sole wealth consisted of a body 6ft. long, a magnificent constitution, a perfect knowledge of farming details, a clear conscience, a character pure and unstained, an age of twenty-five years, and last, though perhaps his richest possession, his young wife, Mary, a perfect helpmeet, beaming all over with true Irish good humour, and fully determined to make the best of the new and very strange land.

Tim was not long in finding an employer. His frank honest face attracted the notice of a young sheep farmer at Bathurst Plains, then on a trip to Sydney (when his wool got down), to lay in a stock of supplies to be sent back by the bullock teams, and to hire just such a servant as Tim. A few words, and Tim was engaged to cross the Blue Mountains to his new home and field of usefulness. We need not enter fully into his feelings on this journey. but we may depend upon it that the mountain air produced that feeling of exhilaration with which we are so familiar ; and I fancy I can see him now, with his long frieze coat, his old " caubeen," on his head, (in the band of which is stuck the black " dudeen"), his

stick, a real blackthorn, under his left arm, as he
marches proudly along—a sense of genuine independence unknown to him in the "ould counthry"
beginning to push its way into his now thankful heart,
feeling that at length he had escaped the misery and
wretchedness of the country he had left behind, with all
its crushing, hopeless penury.

At that time a state of things existed here which has,
happily, long since passed away. All society was
divided into two classes—those who came somewhat
unwillingly, and those who, like Tim, had the proud
satisfaction of knowing that they "came out in their
own boots." The first class, strange to say, considering
all the circumstances, and being in a majority, began to
imagine that the whole country was made for them
alone, and looked upon the "Jimmygrants" (with an
expletive)—as newcomers were called—as intruders,
and to be treated with hatred and contempt.

When Tim reached his master's home, he found most
of his fellow-servants to be this class. He soon learned
to know that his advent among them was looked upon
with anything but favour. He was at once sent to
Coventry. Practical jokes, jeering remarks, and a
hundred other unpleasantnesses, made him feel that his
absence was preferred to his company. Some of the
men in the same service had "come out free," as Tim
heard, but were so craven in spirit as to claim a share
in crimes they had never committed, in order to secure
immunity from the torment which our friend had to
endure. However, a crisis came about, to use Tim's
own words, in this way :—" One day I had to go to the
creek for some wather, and as I was comin' up the hill
wid the buckets who should come down right forninst
me but Pat Flynn, the Dubliner. He was one of the
'ould hands.' 'Tim,' says he, 'is that clane wather ye
have there?' 'It is,' says I ; 'do ye want a dhrink av

it ? ' for I was always civil to the chaps, for all the chyacking' they gave me. 'It's clane now, says he, bringing his hand from behind his back, and, saving yer presence! putting a handful of wet cowdung into one of the buckets, and then wid a loud laff off he goes.' 'Ye are not done wid me yet, my fine man,' says I to myself, 'big as you are,' for he was a great strappin' lump of a fellow. Well, I takes the wathur up just as it was and I goes off to the hayloft, where I had a couple of propsticks for the dray. When I kim back to the hut there was Pat grinnin' all over his face at the dirty thrick he played me.' 'Pat,' says I, 'ye're a Dubliner, and maybe know how to use the shtick. Take yer chice av thim and come outside wid me, for the divil a one of us will lave this till I get satisfaction out of ye for the insult ye done me this day.' He began to change his face, and to look white and frightened-like, and would not take the shtick from me. So I began to get warm-like, an' I thrun 'em on the flure, and says I, "Take yer chice of the shticks, man, and don't stand thrim-lin' there like a coward.' He never made a move, and sein' he was only a cur afther all, I picked up the shticks, and, saving yer presence! I shpit on them, and jist dthrew 'em that way, right and left, across his lip, under his nose. 'Now, Pat, my man,' sez I, 'ye won't play sich thricks on me again.' Well, no man was better plazed wid what I done than the master, and the next time he seen Flynn he gave him a great chaffin' about me, and the end it was he made me farm overseer over the lot of them and I had pace from that time out."

·II.—LAUGHING BILLY.

When I took charge of the station as its manager I found among the native blacks employed there one who was called Laughing Billy. Struck by his large lumi-

L

nous laughter-loving eyes and his good-humoured pleasant expression, I appointed him then and there to be my special attendant, to be my aide-de-camp and galloper; a strong feeling of friendship sprung up between us. Billy was always my mate in scouring the run when mustering the cattle. Like all the black lads of his age, he was a fearless rider, and was very useful, as he had a good knowledge of the country, and that instinctive quality that never allowed him to feel astray no matter how perplexing the monotonous sameness of the scrubby forests seem to be to the weaker intuitive perceptions of the whites. The greater part of Billy's time was passed in trying to stifle convulsive fits of laughter. He could find amusement in everything, thence his name. His good disposition was shown by the affection he always had for his old horse Dodger, or "Storgent," as Billy called him, that being the nearest approach he was able to make to the word. It was a real grief to him to see any of the station hands on Dodger's back. A strong remonstrance was always made when such desecration was dared. Unlike some of his people there was nothing of the beau in his composition. He had a soul above buttons and bootlaces, and a new suit of clothes soon became rags and tatters on him. His gentleness and good humour much more than compensated for his lack of care of personal adornment. No one thought the worse of him for his unconcern in this regard. Billy, by force of circumstances, had hitherto been a home-keeping youth. He had some little desire to see more of white men's ways and manners, and was despatched to help to drive a mob of fat cattle to the nearest large town (Bathurst), some 200 miles away. Here he was to remain for a time until I joined him, when we were to travel back again to the station together. When I did come I was shocked to see the change that had come over my poor friend. He was evidently attacked by that fell disease, consumption, which has proved so fatal to so many of his people.

A kind lady friend, the wife of a medical man (he of the hundredweight of gold), had taken Billy under her charge, and was nursing him at her own house with all attention and tenderness. When I came to see him he was lying on a bed on the floor of a room, comfortably provided for. A native black has a natural disinclination to sleep anywhere except upon the solid earth. As I bent over him he grasped my hand with both his, and his great eyes (appearing doubly large from his shrunken features) looked at me most piteously and inquiringly, as though to learn from me what it all meant. His natural mirth had all gone, and a spiritualized seriousness had taken its place. I tried to cheer him up by news of his station friends, and the hope that he would soon join them. He was not to be deceived by any such delusive hope. The dignity of death was upon him, and he looked as though he felt that a sublime and altogether new experience was soon to be his. The expectancy of the hidden and uncertain future, darkly guessed at, blotted out all interest in the present, and the past. Soon the day came round when I knew that a grave must be made. Moved by what may be looked upon as a foolish sentiment, but in recalling which after a third of a century, I feel no sense of shame, I determined that none but myself should perform the last act of friendship, feeling that his ever ready and unselfish attention to me demanded so much, at least, at my hands at a time when no other service was possible. I chose a shapely "uar" tree, and under the shade of its branches I dug his grave and placed him therein, with his face to the setting sun, towards the land of his own people. When all was ready, a few standing round with uncovered heads, we prayed, "God be merciful to him." When the last

L2

sad act was finished, we left him there in the sure
hope that the Great Maker of All would, with infinite
love and compassion, deal tenderly with his untutored
but gentle and guileless soul.

III.—DENIS McGUIRE.

The fatherland of Denis was easily told: the pure
brogue of his speech marked it unmistakably. He was
the stockman manager of a cattle-station; he was a
well-made middle-sized man. Small, sharp grey eyes,
somewhat deep-set under beetle brows, and thin, closely
compressed lips, marked a determined character. When
he spoke, his words came with a certain decision and
deliberation, not to say affectation of force. The most
trivial sentences were emphasised in the same manner,
as though the greatest importance attached to the
utterance of them. His face was speckled all over with
small dark blue spots. This branding happened in this
way: Denis and his wife Bridget—a tall, gaunt, but
kind and hospitable woman in her way—were travelling
up the country and camping out as they went. One
rainy day, as they turned out for dinner, the wood was
wet and the wife was long in starting the fire. Denis,
having returned to the camp after hobbling his horses
away on a bit of good feed, feeling cold and hungry and
seeing that the fire, with its subsequent pot of hot tea,
was not much advanced, said sharply, "Whoy can't ye
make the fire burn?" "The wood is wet, and iverything is wet, and that's why," says she. "Get the
flashk of powdther from the cart and pour some of the
powdther on, and ye'll soon have a blaze." "Faith,"
says Bridget, "I'll do nothing of the sort; I don't
onderstand them things." "Och," says he, with scorn
at her womanly timidity and natural dread of anything
connected with firearms, "Give the flashk to me." The

flask was full, and, striking a manly attitude in reproach of his wife's want of courage, and to exhibit his own superior knowledge and indifference to all danger, he began to pour the powder on the now slowly-smouldering fire. In an instant there was a loud explosion, and Denis had lost all the skin from his face and all the hair from his head, and was indelibly branded, as the grains of the powder became inextricably buried in his flesh. Denis used to admit afterwards that there was some " sinse in the ould woman afther all."

He had a great fright one day.   To use his own word, " It was in the toime of the bad drooth, I wanted to git some grassh for my horse, so I takes a rapin hook and goes under the bank of the river where the cattle could not get at some that was growing there.   As soon as I cuts a good arrmful I puts the hook ondthur it to lift it aff the ground, when a shnake dhrops out av it, aud that minute I feels shomething shting me on the leg.   Be jaberz, sez I to meself, I believe I am bit wid a shnake, and me hearrt wid one jump lept clane up into my mouth.   Well, I studies to see what I'd best do, and I goes to the blacks' camp where big Yarree the black-fellow was, and I sez 'Yarree,' sez I, 'I believe I am bit wid a shnake,' and all the time I could scarcely shpake for the way my hearrt was choking me in the throat.   'Where, like it,' sez he.   I pulls up my trousers to show the place on the calf of my leg.   Well Yarree looks at it and he gives a great laff.   He sez, sez he, ' That fellow only ant, and little fellow ant too,' and with that laff my hearrt fell clane out of my mouth and dropped down into the waist of my breeches."

Our friend sometimes turned an honest penny as a dealer in horseflesh.   A buyer appeared one day, and to a question he replied, " Have I horrse for sale ? Faith thin I have one as fat as mud, and as quite as a sheep, and at the same time, mind ye, he's full of sperrit. He's a great animal intoirely. He's what ye'd call a raal powdtherin' horse" (great emphasis on " powd-therin' "). "Go inside and the ould woman will git ye something to ate, and I'll send the blackfellow for the horse." While " the ould woman " entertains the stranger, Denis goes to the camp. " Boney," says he, " go and catch the yellow bay and bring him up to the hut, but before ye fetch him, Boney, take him down into the bed of the river, and take a big sthick wid ye, Boney, and whelt him well ; knock the d——l into him, Boney ; make him so as he'll jump out of his skin if ye only look at him." Boney obeys instructions, and when the horse is brought for inspection after the treatment he has received, he is, from fear, all life and movement. A bargain is struck and the brute is led away. As the new owner gets out of hearing, Denis, with his legs apart and his hands sunk down into his trousers pockets, crumpling the notes there to make sure that he has got twice the value, with a grim smile on his face, is heard to mutter, " I am well rid of ye any way. Of all the sluggish brutes I ever threw a leg over, that wretch bates them all ; a man might just as well ride a pig. May shweet bad luck go wid ye !"

IV.—Fishhook.

When Governor Sir Charles Fitzroy came to visit Bathurst in 1847, one of the public institutions he in-spected was the gaol. In it was a prisoner, a black-fellow from the Bogan, who was supposed to have committed some depredation there. He could speak little or no English, and was altogether wild and savage. There was no interpreter at the trial, so that the whole proceeding was mere dumb show to him. He belonged to the Wongaibun (Redant) tribe. He called himself **Peeshoo,** a name altered by the whites to Fishhook.

My father (who was then a member of the first elected Council for a large country district and the Governor's host) begged for liberty for Fishhook, and promised to take care of him. The governor inquired into the case, and as there were grave doubts as to the guilt of the prisoner, the evidence of identity (strange to say, often the weakest evidence) being not at all strong, he was liberated. A policeman brought him to my father's place. Poor fellow! He was let out of gaol just in time to save his reason. Like some wild animal, he was too old and much too settled in savage habits to understand the confinement and discipline and to him the terrible solitude of the prison. It was a restraint and mode of life that his imagination could not have had the remotest conception of. It was no wonder, then, that when he came to us his reason was tottering. A little longer in confinement, and he must have become a raving maniac. He was always believed by his new master to have been perfectly innocent of the crime laid to his charge. He was clothed and fed, but for a considerable time little could be made of him. He was apparantly full of revenge for the wrongs done to him. He used to take his stand on the brow of a hill, and shout and gesticulate and throw imaginary weapons, and spit in the direction of his gaolers for hours every day. Now and again he would throw off all his clothes, and at such times he was altogether a fearful and terrific object, and would take no notice of any people belonging to his new home, but would walk rapidly past them with light springing step, his hands clenched, and muttering incoherently. However, time, liberty and kindness worked wonders, and when he grew calmer and more rational, he became very useful. He lived with us for some fifteen years until he died, and during all that time had no desire to go back to his own part of the country, but gradually conformed to somewhat civilised habits. A small room was assigned to him, which he shared with his dogs. He learned to boil and bake for himself, kept his room tolerably swept and clean, washed and mended his own clothes and always had a clean rig out for Sundays. A looking-glass, comb and razor were adjuncts to his toilet. It was a sight to see him shaving, as he rasped his stubbled chin with a dull edge that brought tears into his eyes again. After such painful cleansing he appeared quite "a swell." He was entrusted with a horse and cart, and used to cut and draw wood and take the weekly rations round to the sheep stations. He was much attached to his horse, and always kept him well fed and in good order.

For a long time he resisted, from disinclination to the taste, the use of strong liquors, but the bad habits and example of the "old hands" among his fellow-servants was too much for him, and he learned to take his glass and another one, with as much gusto as any civilized Christian can do his whisky. At length he became ill, and though medical attention, and female tenderness and nursing were bestowed on him, he was shortly laid beside Laughing Billy. If anything were wanting to show it, I venture to think his life and story conclusively prove the common origin of the human race. There was nothing foreign to humanity in him.

A SUICIDE'S GRAVE.

IT was after one of those long seasons of drought which are so periodically prevalent in the pastoral districts of New South Wales. To him who has lived through one of these dry spells on the spot nothing can be so hopeless and depressing. Nothing makes one feel so utterly helpless and unable. The drought of 1862 will long be remembered on the Lachlan for its severity. Several previous years had been very good. The year '60 was specially favorable. Long green grass was to be seen all the year through. An unusually moist summer made new arrivals think that the seasons had changed. Said they, " We shall never see droughts again." The older residents who had seen '38 and '39, and again '49 and '50, used to shake their heads and look wise, and tell the stories of the past. They were looked upon as antique fossils. " Was not the whole country becoming stocked ? Tanks and dams were being made. Nature was adapting herself in some mysterious or perhaps specially providential way to the new requirements of the country." This argument had little effect upon the fossils. They still shook their heads. " We shall see," said they. Some of the more sanguine of the " New Chum " squatters seriously thought that because by means of tanks they had conserved a few thousand gallons of water, the evaporation of these would supplement the natural supply in sufficient quantity to make droughts a thing of the past. The year of '61 was a fairly prosperous one, but notwithstanding the tanks, the rainfall had decreased considerably. However, a great increase of stock took place. Every animal old enough to fatten was sent to market and the butcher's shambles. Whether or not they preferred this kind of death to that nature might have given them, I have been unable to learn. Good rains fell in October, and the rivers were all full. Now dry-westerly winds blew sharply in November and parched up the herbage. The summer was dry throughout, with its hot and cold spells, the thermometer going up to 110deg. in the shade, and sometimes falling as low as 65deg. in 48 hours, when cyclones, accompanied by clouds and dust and a few drops of rain, were passing, February and March having failed to give rains of any value, stock began to fall off in condition as the plains became bare of grass. A few showers in the winter sent the stock out into the back country and produced a slight growth in the herbage. When September came there was some little greenness to be seen, and hopes revived as a fresh came down the river. These hopes were not realised, and were doomed to complete disappointment, as October set in dry and dusty. To add a last straw to the camel's back, myriads of locusts began to come up out of the ground; small, tiny black specks at first, and growing rapidly, they destroyed every vestige of green that the slight rains of springtime had caused to grow; and when they assumed their wings they filled the air as thick as a snowstorm, and hosts of them were drowned in the river, covering the water with a stinking layer of their dead bodies, and providing a great feed for the fish. The ibis, too, came in thousands to feed upon the locusts, and deserve all protection in consequence. And now the cattle, as the backwater completely dried up, began to march into the river to water in long dust-raising files, slowly moving across the plains. And the heated air rises and quivers under the hot sun, and the cattle loom

large in the delusive mirage which seems to cover the
plains with glassy sheets of water.

Cattle always go to water along pathways which they
make by walking in single file. A natural instinct
directs the movement. Many hundreds may water at a
small pond. But to do this they come to it in droves of
20 or 30 at a time. Each drove when satisfied marches
off, and by that time another is close by to take the
place. They begin to water at about 5 o'clock in the
evening, and come in relays till daylight or sunrise.
Before fencing was adopted, watching cattle coming to
water by moonlight, and keeping in custody all that
came, was a good plan to secure those that could not
be got by other means. Old bullocks that lived away
out in the back scrubs and eluded pursuit, were captured
in this way. It was a spirit-stirring and dangerous
business, many of the cattle were very wild, and made
desperate efforts to escape, and the holey ground often
brought man and horse down in crashing falls at full
gallop. As December, 1861, was dry and the grass
was all gone, the older and weaker of the cattle began
to stick in the mud at the water's edge in the rivers and
lagoons, and die there. Towards the end of the month
the stronger began to fail, as all the scrub, the yarran
trees, the warriah bushes, the salt bushes, and indeed
every green thing within reach had been devoured. In
January the poor brutes began to die in their camps
away from the water. On the surface of the plains
there was nothing but dust. All the water holes stank
with dead cattle. Hundreds could be counted at
favorite watering-places. Dead cattle could be seen
everywhere ; indeed, one might ride for miles, and dead
cattle were always in sight. And still the sky glittered
in its beautiful blue depths, while the heated air,
radiating from the black and dusty land, rose upwards
continually in quivering undulations.

On the first day of February the canvas bag full of water hanging under the verandah of the station hut showed outwardly a moist surface. There is a feeling in the air somewhat different from usual. A gentle wind is commencing to blow from the northward; clouds are appearing in that direction, and long mares' tails (cirrus clouds) are spreading themselves in fanlike figures over the sky from the westward. As the day goes on the clouds thicken, and a low bank of vapour appears in the west, behind which the sun disappears, and is not seen when he really sets below the horizon. The clouds still drift overhead from the north, and when night comes a few pattering drops of rain are heard on the shingled roof, and then cease. Our hearts are in our mouths. We dare not speak for fear the expression of a hope might have the effect of dispersing the clouds, for our hopes have long indeed been deferred into heart-sickness. But hark! another little shower, brisker and longer than the last, and in an hour or so a steady, gentle rain is falling, and is even beginning to drip from the eaves. We go to bed, but not to sleep. We are up and down all night wandering out into the verandah, standing on the very edge in naked feet and peering out into the darkness. How sweet is the scent of the moistened earth! How soothing is the constant soft murmur of the falling rain! How refreshing the splash from the eavesdrops upon our feet! Thank God, it has come at last. Our eyes fill with tears of thankfulness. We feel that we can scarcely trust ourselves to speak, lest we should be unmanned and begin to cry. Next day the wind shifted round to the eastward, and the rain comes in heavy, continuous driving showers. All the small water-courses run strong streams, and the low grounds begin to fill. Near sundown there is a sudden lull, and a great black bank of clouds appears in the west and comes rolling on overhead,

and then the rain that has fallen seems as nothing compared with the torrent from this cloud, which pours
from the roof in perfect waterspouts. This at length
passes by and there are intermittent showers during the
rest of the night. The morning is light and cool, with
a gentle south-west wind, and the face of the country is
all bare mud and sheets of water, and in a few hours a
little green tinge is to be seen here and there, and in a
few days there is a great change visible in the appearance of the country as the grass appears to grow. The
cattle left all wander away into the back country. How
many died we never knew, at least a third, possibly a
half. The increase from July, 1861 (before the drought)
to July, 1862, one year, was 1700. The increase from
July, 1862, to October, 1864 (after the drought), over
two years, was only 1600. The eight dry weeks from
December 1 to January 31, did all the mischief. If two
inches had fallen in November after the locusts took
wing, no losses would have been. We only saved two
milking cows out of 23, and these were kept alive by
cutting boughs for them to eat. On March 1 a storm,
identical in character with the one four weeks previous,
visited the place, and then the grass grew a foot high
and more all over the country. Some 10 inches of rain
had probably fallen in these two storms. The winter
following was wet and the river was in constant flood,
running bank high for weeks together. The managing
partner's cottage is near the bank of the river. It is
built of sawn pine slabs, and has a shingled roof and
boarded floor and ceilings. Its walls inside are covered
with calico and paper. There are wide verandahs on
two sides. To the posts are trained grape vines and
dolichos and the beautifully fragile maurandia, with
dark purple velvet flowers. Rose bushes and chrysan-
themums and oleanders, when in flower, add brightness
to the little flower-garden in front. Inside, the place is,

for a bush home, comfortably furnished, and one corner
of the sitting-room is occupied by a good collection of
books.   The country around is level and flat.   The outlook is across an open plain through which the river
meanders in graceful serpentine windings, with its high
leafy wall of blue gums.   Out from the river the country
is prettily broken by open plains, fringed and dotted
with myall trees and bounded by forests and clumps of
box and pine and belar.   In the distance is to be seen
a low range of hills relieving the level monotony by their
undulating blue outlines.   A great stockyard, 6ft. high,
and enclosing about 3a. of ground, stands on a small
hillock of red soil at the edge of the plain.   As the herd
of cattle on the run did number, before the drought,
some 6000 head, a large yard was necessary for its
working.

The month of August had nearly passed, and the
spring was setting in, the plains were beginning to look
quite green.   At night, in the sitting-room of the
cottage, the station manager and a friend are playing
a quiet game of cards.   In an easy chair is the house-
wife busy with her needle, making those little garments,
which, to an experienced eye, are somewhat prophetic.
As she works, her mind seems to be in deep reverie, as
the regular and ceaseless click of needle is repeated with
mechanical precision.   Her thoughts are in the future,
with the conjectures of the forms and features of that
first little one, which in the fancy of a mother's love in
tender imagination she presses to her bosom and endows
with every charm and grace.   The station life to her is
a very solitary one.   There is no neighbour, except the
servants, nearer than some ten miles away.   She has
married the man of her choice, however, and is determined cheerfully and courageously to perform her duty
with a hope that prosperous years may enable them to
choose a less unsociable home.   The rain without pours

down in relentless torrents. Would that it had only come when it was more wanted! As we wondered when the drought was going to end, so now, we think almost with fear, that the rain will never cease—unsatisfied mortals that we are. The lamp on the table illuminates the room, and the three-log myallwood fire burns fiercely and brightly with its pretty pale rose-colored slender flame.

The manager's friend is a cattle - buyer from Melbourne. He is an educated, intellectual gentleman. He has had misfortunes, and must do something for a living. He has had much practical experience of bushcraft, and knows fat cattle when he sees them. His latest venture was to pioneer the Gawler Rangers, and endeavour to form a large sheep station there. Droughts and unforseen expenses consequent thereupon swallowed up all the capital of self and partner, and sent them both adrift to seek other means of making money. Christian O—— was Scotch by birth, and claimed to be the rightful heir to a Scottish Earldom held in abeyance. "When I make my fortune," said he, " I will establish my claim." He died before this could be carried out. He had been educated at one of the great historical English Public schools, and had all the fine, independent manly tone of that training. A love of adventure—and finding no opening for his energies in the overcrowded condition of the old country—brought him to Australia. He had been a private secretary for a short time to the first Anglican Bishop of Australia. Had tried squatting in the days before the gold discovery. Had sold out of that business. Had speculated and lost all his capital. Had been obliged to work as a bullock driver. Had managed large pastoral properties for others. Was now on the wrong side of 50, a tall, lithe, active, sanguine man still, with nothing but colonial experience and an unblemished reputation as his only properties. A kind and friendly man, he was not without little sarcastic touches for his best friends, laid on with such good humour and sparkling twinkle of the eye as made the victims like him all the better for his candid openness. He was a rolling stone, and attrition with his fellows added some little roughnesses to his character. As honest as the sun and rather close in his dealings, one felt quite safe in striking a bargain with him. Melbourne agents trusted his personal integrity and advanced money to any extent for his purchases. With few, if any, strong religious convictions, he had a conscience so refined as to stand much in the way of his worldly success. He once obtained a lucrative Government appointment which he could, at his own discretion, treat as a sinecure or not, as it so pleased him. His temperament forbade him to be inactive. After a time he voluntarily resigned his position and his daily bread, because he found that he was not able to do the good he anticipated. So there he was, another Australian antipodean anomaly, a man with education and abilities for much higher possibilities, driven by an inexorable fate or crass perverseness to drive bullocks to market for a living.

While the game goes on, the fire burns brightly, and the rain stills pours outside with chilling persistence, and the friends discuss the prospects of the season, and the land law lately passed. O—— takes the popular views, and hopes much from the settlement of the country by a small proprietary. The other, whose whole interests and heartstrings are bound up in the place (it has been his home for some years), who knows every tree on the run, every romantic little nook among the hills, whose delight has been to watch his cattle fattening on the plains with all the profitable consequences, and who has come to look upon the river as a live thing and a friend, who, as a schoolboy, was taught to look forward with ambitious pleasure to the time when the management should devolve upon him—as is most natural—is much stirred with antagonism to the future prospects, and cannot look with complacency upon the advent of strangers whose claims may mean ruin to him, while hurling him from the little throne which custom has taught him to look upon as inseparable from himself. The day after, driving showers from the south-west alternate with gleams of sunshine; but the next day is bright and clear. Early in the morning the son of a neighbouring squatter comes to tell the manager, who is a magistrate, that he has found the dead body of a man lying in the bush. A messenger is dispatched to the nearest police-station, ten miles away. A flooded ana-branch of the river has to be crossed before the body can be seen, so "Jackey Street" and "Laughing Billy," two of the station blacks, are dispatched to cut a canoe at the point nearest to the spot. These canoes are sheets of bark, stripped from the bole of a large slightly-bent tree. If skilfully taken off, they make efficient and useful vessels. As the party is complete, they start off with pick and spade and axe, and, lastly, a prayer-book. They do not like to consign a fellow-creature to the grave without some of the usual reverential practice. When the ana-branch is reached, the men and saddles are ferried over in the canoe, and then the horses are made to swim across the stream, which they do readily, with much snorting and blowing. The country passed over is diversified open plain and woodland. All the hollow depressions are now small lakelets, with wild ducks innumerable upon them. The plains are green with young grass, and in a month's time will be patterned carpet-like with large informal blotches of colour, as the yellow, white, and blue flowers come into bloom. Native-companions dance and make love with ridiculous antic awkwardness in the propitious season,

M

and the wild turkeys strut about and swell their necks
with amorous self-conceit—that is if we may judge them
from the known foibles of the human race. But perhaps
this is too hard upon the bird. The men chat and
laugh and chaff each other, as they ride along splashing
through the shallow sheets of water left by the late rain.
As the guide indicates that they near the spot, a silence
falls upon them. Death exacts the respect due to him.

At length, at a little distance through some park-like
trees, and on an open place, a dark object unlike anything else but the thing it is, is seen lying on the green
grass. The body is that of a tall, thin, grey-headed old
man, stretched at full length on his back on the wet
ground. His arms lie close by his side, his few grey
locks wave and quiver in the gentle breeze. The half-
shut sightless eyes stare blindly up to heaven. As the
men ride up to the body and gather around it, their
horses sniff and snort at and start back from it. They
dismount and tie their horses to the trees, and proceed
to examine and if possible discover the cause of death.
A pair of well-worn blankets are huddled in a heap close
by, and there is a large bag with a bundle in it.
Apparently the man had camped here for some
day or two, as there is a large heap of ashes of a fire by
which he lies, evidently extinguished by the rain. On
the heap of ashes lie a knife, a razor and a whetstone.
They are about concluding that it is a case of death
from want and exposure (as the small bags in which he
has carried some food are quite empty), when one, more
curious than the rest, tenderly draws down the neck
from under the right jaw a large knot of a thick woollen
comforter. "Good God," he exclaims, "the man's
throat is cut!" Here, then, was the cause of death.
They then gathered from the indications that the poor
old man was lost, that his scanty provisions had failed
him, that the heavy night's rain over which they had

rejoiced, had so completely exhausted him that he had been unable to keep his fire burning, and had taken a short way to end his worldly troubles. There was deliberation, too, in the method. He had taken the razor and discarded it for some reason. He had then sharpened the knife, and with one stroke severed the jugular vein, and so died. His very last act showed most . pathetically that he must have been somewhat ashamed and repentant. He had evidently drawn over the part from which his life was flowing away the large double knot of the woollen comforter, as if to hide the signs of his guilt. Gold enough was found on him to have purchased provisions, had they been obtainable. Papers found in his bundle disclosed a sad case. He had been employed by some wealthy squatters as a night-watcher of sheep. His pay was less than 9d. per day. In the judgment of his employers he had failed in his duty. He had been summoned to appear at the court to show cause why his munificent wages should not be forfeited for the masters' benefit. He had thereupon wandered away with the intention of disobeying the summons and leaving his masters to do what they liked with his hardly-earned pittance. These masters had claimed the pound of flesh, and, with better fortune than Shylock had, at last obtained the blood as well. The magistrate took the evidence of the finder of the body, and of the constable who examined it. Then the blacks cut a sheet of bark, and a grave was dug under two beautiful cypress trees, and the body laid within the bark was placed in it, and· they all stood round the grave with uncovered heads, while a portion of the English burial service was read. As they covered him over with the damp earth, a gentle shower drifted from the westward and fell upon them. And the grave being filled, they rode away for some short distance, when the sun shone out in all his brightness from under the dark cloud, and as they took a last look at the scene of their sad work, a beautiful and perfect rainbow was arched over the spot. The two cypress trees were lit up in full relief against the black raincloud slowly drifting to the east, and they reflected a light—beryl-hued—and sparkled in brilliant splendour with raindrops as with diamonds. As the men gazed, a gentle breeze, softly sighing, shook the drops in glistening tears upon the grave. And the trees, standing under the very centre of the bow, seemed, with their delicate fragile tops, to point upwards, like angels' fingers, to the glorious iridescence, and to assure the onlookers of a bright material morrow for themselves, and to give (for who can tell?) a heavenly promise of a brighter spiritual dawning for that poor friendless castaway lying darkly in his lonely grave.

MY EXPERIENCE AS A HOSPITAL COLLECTOR.

"COME with me to-morrow," said a friend; I promise you a day of healthy exercise, a good appetite for your dinner, some little amusement, and a feeling of conscious rectitude, with something to reflect upon after the day's work is over." "How may a poor dyspeptic secure so many remedies for his complaint?" said I. "By simply coming with me through the district of this city allotted to me to collect money in for our hospital."

It was agreed, and on the following morning I presented myself at my friend's door. It was a cold, raw, foggy winter's early day. For here in Australia, at 2000ft. above the sea, we really have a season that may be dignified by the name of winter. " A bad day," said I; "people cannot be charitible in such weather." However, with better omen, the sun soon burst through the mists in warming splendour. The thick fog rolled away in dense masses, and contracting into cloudlets, finally disappeared. A calm, crisp, bright blue day followed. A smart walk soon brought us to the boundary of our district and sent the blood flowing rapidly and glowing through our veins, and filled us with a very kindly and good-humoured sense of our undertaking. Our system was to ask at every door, no matter how unpromising the outlook might be. It was the right plan. By doing so small surprises were in store for us. Those who gave seemed to have a gratified pleasure in the bestowal. Those who could not give were not always displeased at our request.

We knocked at the first door. After a shuffling of startled feet, a woman's voice behind the door asked in strong Irish accent, " What do ye want? Who's there?" " Oh, white men," said my friend. A narrow strip of light as the door opened shone on a very rubicund face and dirty, shabby exterior generally. We explain our errand. " I've nothing for ye," said she, as she slammed the door and dashed a puff of very malodourous air against us. Not a very cheering beginning.

The next place was a Chinese store, smelling horribly or fragrantly of opium smoke. Stretched on a couch behind the counter was a Chinaman in full puff of the burning aromatic gum. I must confess I like the smell of opium smoke. Somehow it has a disinfecting suggestion about it not at all unpleasant. In Chinese quarters it is the sweetest odour one meets with, and seems to be the right thing in the right place. After a little pleasant chaff with two or three Johnnies in the shop—I never can address a Chinaman without laughing, they are very provocative of mirth—a thin shrivelled old man (the boss), with a good-natured expression in his face, came in, and without much discussion cheerfully gave us a guinea. We call at another little shop, and knocking at the counter several times without attracting anyone's attention, I bawled out "Shop." This brought out a stout old lady, with unkempt hair and somewhat untidy dress, with a merry twinkle in her eye, however, slightly reassuring. She waddled into the room, shambling along in loosely-slippered feet, followed by her husband. He had evidently been long drilled into giving her the *pas.* "What do ye want making all that noise? Are ye police wid a warrant, or what are ye, at all at all?" Our business explained, "Divil a ha'porth I have in the house," said she, turning to a shelf and commencing to turn over and rummage among a number of small empty boxes, in which she pretended the money was kept. "Have you not got a stocking somewhere?" said I. "Faith I have," says she, "with a leg in it." Then turning to her husband she put her hand into her pocket, and, pulling out a well-worn, greasy old purse, said to him, "How much shall I give them? Half-a-crown?" "Give 'em five shillings," said he. "Five shillings!" said she, lifting up her hands in an expression of holy horror at the awfully insane spirit of charitable lavishment that had suddenly overcome her "old man," and looking at him slowly from head to foot, in unfeigned astonishment, to see whether or not he had not taken clean leave of his senses. "Five shillings!" The old man, to his credit, looked firm and resolute, and gave her a nod of confirmation of his intention. So with a sigh and a "Tut! tut! tut!" the money was slowly counted shilling by shilling and dropped, apparently very unwillingly, into my friend's hand.

A wretchedly dirty, squalid, almost completely un-furnished place was opened by a pretty-looking young woman, with some little attempt at tidiness and neat-ness in the arrangement of her scanty clothing.   As we stood in the doorway, we saw a young man cowering over a miserable fire.   We stated our calling.   " I've nothing for you," said he, somewhat sadly.   " I only came out of gaol this morning ; I'm always in gaol ; the police take good care of that ; they never give me a chance."   We were about to turn away, when the girl, still holding the door, put her hand into her dress pocket, and taking it out again, with modest timidity tendered a shilling.   Poor girl !   I felt we were very mean to take it ; but perhaps it was better for her that we did. There was so much less for her companion to drink ; and who knows but that the shilling, like the widow's mite, may figure with much compound interest when the last long reckoning is made.

Two incidents stood out in strong contrast.   At one house—the residence of a widow—a little child servant girl answered the door.   She had a plain little face, but bright withal.   She was evidently not unacquainted with hard work.   As I looked at her, the Marchioness in the " Old Curiosity Shop " at once came into my memory.   " Oh ! yes," said she very cheerily ; " I'll give you something, I can give you a shilling ;" and she ran off to get it.   " Whose is this," said I, looking at the coin ; " yours or your mistress's ?"   " Oh ! mine," said she, with a smile full of charitable good humour.   How could I have for a moment doubted it ?   So I entered her name on the list.   " God love the child !" said I to my friend ; "that shilling is more blessed than the five guineas we had from the bank."   At another house a little boy about six years of age came to answer our summons at the door. "Is your father or mother at home?" said I. "No," said he; "they are gone out." I asked his name. Having told me, "What do you want?" said he. I stated our business. "Oh!" said he, with a very serious air, "you had better go next door; we never give to the 'orspital. Oh! no; we don't give to the 'orspital." With a hearty laugh at this young gentleman's precocious harshness, hoping that the idea was all his own, we continued our journeying. We knock at the doors of "cottages of gentility," and are sometimes refused. But at one place, a little distance back from the road, a small hut stood. No sign of wealth, but of sheer poverty pervaded the surroundings. As I stand at the door waiting its opening, I notice two little narrow, well-tended garden beds along the wall and under the drip from the roof. They are thickly overgrown with flowering plants. As this is their season, the violets shed their sweet perfume in the air. While I waited I thought of the truth of that saying of Gladstone's, "that the human heart with infinite pathos always clings to the beautiful forms of flowers," and drew a good augury from the evidence I saw of it before me. The door opened. I gathered from a glimpse of the interior and her appearance, that the mistress was a widow and a washerwoman. There are coloured prints on the walls, of the Crucifixion and the Virgin Mary, and such as devout Roman Catholics like to have ever before them. I tell my errand and ask for a subscription, not, however, without a feeling of meanness, and wonder at the audacity of such a request in such a quarter. "Faith, then, I will," said she, in gentle accents, soft and low, and with a most pleasant, sweet and kindly expression beaming from her face; "it's very good of ye to give up yer time gathering money for them poor crathurs up there," nodding towards the institution not very far away. "It's a raal pleasure to give something for that place; iverything is so clane and so well looked afther there." "I thank you very much," said I, as she put a coin into my hand, quite as much, I feel sure, as she could afford. "That is the pleasantest speech we have heard to-day." "Faith, thin, ye're quite welcome; I only wish I could give ye more." If "the Lord" indeed "loveth a cheerful giver," then this poor widow is not without affections from the right place. "May the odour of her unostentatious sacrifice, sweeter than the scent of her modest violets, find a pleased acceptance at the throne of grace," is my humble prayer.

On application at one store, of which the keeper, to judge from appearances, seemed well to do, we were offered a half-crown. Last year the donation from here was five shillings. A merry-looking young Chinaman was standing at the counter. At sight of the half-crown he burst into a fit of laughter. "You only gib hap-a-clown; me allays gib one guinea long a ospittal," said he, and off he went again into another "kink" of laughter. We left with one half-a-crown, the Chinaman's merriment still sounding in our ears. After we were some yards away, a little girl came running after us with another half-a-crown from the store. The Chinaman's laughter had had some little effect.

The day passed with varying success. Sums from five guineas to a shilling were received. We walked for five good solid hours and travelled miles, and netted some £25 for the institution. Near sunset we knocked at the last door, that of a rather neat little cottage in the suburbs, with some cultivation ground attached. A very nice-looking, tidily-dressed young lady told us (with somewhat affected alliteration) that "Papa was ploughing in the paddock." We went towards the field, in which we saw a plough and horses, but no man. Looking around we could see no sign of "papa." At length I said "I see him," as I quite suddenly caught sight of a pair of legs slowly disappearing through a hole in the paling boundary fence. "By Jove! I believe he is giving us the slip." I stepped on one side to obtain a view of the other and shady side of the fence, and there sure, enough, I saw our friend slowly draw himself through the palings and lay himself out at full length on the shade, and evidently "playing 'possum." As he stretched himself out as flat as he could, we enjoyed the scene for a few seconds and then hailed him. He refused to give us anything, and in reply to an inquiry as to the state of his health, he told us that he "did not feel very well just then." We could believe it. He had no doubt recognised my friend, who had canvassed the district before. On that previous occasion he gave two shillings, a florin piece. That magnificent donation was not had from him without a good deal of unmerited adverse criticism of the management of the hospital and a hint given that, unless things were altered more in accordance with his ideas of satisfaction, his subscription for the future must cease.

Highly amused at our interview with this very charitable gentleman, we wended our way home into the city as the smoke from the evening fires began to hang over it, and feeling sufficiently tired to make us sure of a good night's rest. With this last as an exception, it was gratifying to find that all applied to admitted that to subscribe to the hospital was very right and proper. If the means in many cases had been proportioned to the will, we would have had our bag better filled. Very few refused who had the means of giving, and many gave to whom the few shillings parted with were a real sacrifice.

A VISIT TO MOUNT WILSON.

WHEN the Great Western Railway was in course of construction, and that portion running along the crown of the Darling Causeway and making a long detour to the northward from the old western traffic road was being made, Mount Wilson was re-discovered. Wooden sleepers were required for the formation of the railroad, and the men employed to procure them made explorations towards the high mountain which from a distance may be noticed to be more densely and loftily wooded than the adjacent hills. They were rewarded not only by the finding of large quantities of valuable timber, but by the discovery of a patch of land which, for climate and richness, is unrivalled in this colony. The authorities, hearing of the place, sent a surveyor to measure the land into portions for sale, and the mountain was named Wilson, after the then Minister of Lands, the late J. B. Wilson. The land was offered by public auction at the town of Windsor on April 25 and 26, 1870, at prices from £1 to £2 10s. per acre. Not one acre of it was then sold. Some time after a gentleman, who now occupies the loveliest spot of the mountain, was in search of a place to erect a mountain residence. He could find plenty of elevation and good air, but good land was scarce in the great sandstone formation. Someone told him of Mount Wilson. He went there, and with considerable pluck and perseverance pushed his way through the dense growth of the place, and finding that the land could be bought by paying down the money at which it had been offered at auction, he purchased 93 acres. Any one who has had the pleasure of visiting Mr. Wynne's place and looking at the view from his verandah, will not begrudge him the reward of his adventure. It seems then to have become known to a favoured few that a "good thing" was to be had at Mount Wilson, and I find in a public record that nearly 1000 acres were taken up by after auction selection sometime before April 23, 1875. Some eight or nine gentlemen have made summer residences on this hill, the beauties of which I will endeavour to describe. I had never seen the place until an old and respected friend gave myself and some members of my family an invitation to spend a few days with him and his family at his cottage there. Starting from Bathurst, we are duly delivered at the Mount Wilson platform by the Western morning up-train. We noticed as we went along that, in this very propitous season, the forest trees are more luxuriant than usual, and that their foliage colours the hill-sides with most delicate greys and light greens, and their topmost tender shoots surround their heads with bright red aureoles. As our mechanical monster puffs and gasps with laboured breath and slow speed up the Lithgow Valley Zig-zag, we see below us the native hawthorn filling the lowest depths with its masses of white blossoms and making a lovely floral glacier, which might almost be mistaken for the snow—the last remnant of a winter's cold—which in appearance it so closely resembles. We are delayed an hour at the platform, some part of which time we "amuse" ourselves with sandwiches and rich ripe apricots and pure mountain rain water. A simple repast, but to my thinking there is nothing more delicious than a cup of cold, clear water after eating luscious fruit. I have no envy for the man who requires his alcoholic stimulant to follow such food. And now

the down train has come, for which my friend's servant
with his waggon had waited for provisions to be
obtained by it; and, oh fate! the daily newspaper and
the post; from these at least one would have hoped to
have been relieved in such a secluded spot.

Now we travel along that old mountain road, long
only known to drovers and shepherds as Bell's New
Line. It was so called after the late Mr. Archibald
Bell, quite recently a member of the Legislative Council,
who, when a young man, discovered this second track
over the mountains. It is much to Bell's credit that he
succeeded starting from the same point—the junction
of the Grose River with the Nepean—as Bass, who
failed, declaring that the mountain range was utterly
impassable. This road winds round mountain sides
more precipitous than a house roof, and occasionally
follows the very crown of a ridge, so narrow that there
is but a small strip of level ground on either side the
track. Probably, no more desolate or inhospitably
barren region lies anywhere than this. But not without
its wild beauties of rocky precipices and almost fathom-
less valleys. " Very gorgeous," as the wretched punster
of the party, not as yet overcome by the sublimity of
the scene, flippantly remarked. And now the track is
narrower as it passes through a grove of closely-growing,
white-stemmed gums, their branches meeting overhead,
throwing a thin, checkered shade on our path. The
ground on either side is covered with great dark-
brown stones—not a blade of grass to be seen. It is
just such a place as should have some dreadful
legend attached to it. It appeared as though in
some long time past an evil enchantment had worked
an everlasting curse upon the spot. As we are thus
thinking of it, a brilliant butterfly flits from stone to
stone, and we realise the fact that there is no place in
the world so poor as not to be enriched by nature's

beautiful adornments. Whether or not the butterfly returned us a similar compliment upon our monstrous and clattering intrusion is not known to me. We see the evidences of a great bush fire, which last summer had swept along the mountain sides, destroying all the smaller vegetation and leaving innumerable charred trunks to testify to its raging character. The poor trees were doing their best to cover their blackened sides and trunks and hide their nakedness with a fresh growth of young green shoots. Thus nature distributes her favours, the destruction of one life often meaning the reviving of another, and plant life thousands of miles away, may build up themselves on their food driven off into the air by this great fire.

At length we leave Bell's Line and proceed along the sandstone leader, which ends with the mass of volcanic capping called Mount Wilson. I wish its native name had not been lost. Flowers innumerable—blue and pink and white and yellow—are seen in little coloured dots to brighten the roadside. I would not weary the reader with their somewhat harsh and ugly botanic names, even if I were able. I can only hope that in time they will all be known by some homely, tender and descriptive nomenclature, which will characterise their qualities and native beauties, and make them as much things of the heart as of scientific tongues.

And now we see before us, through the scanty foliage, a bold hill rising some 300ft. above us, covered with a more luxuriant growth, and soon we are at the foot of a steep ascent, where the immediate difference in soil and vegetation is most marked. Beautiful acacias (with dark green feathery leaves) and mint-trees, covered with snowy pink-tipped blossoms, and whitening the roadway with their falling petals, tree-ferns completely shading the ground with their graceful green fronds, and making symmetrical pedestals for the great columnar gums and sassafras trees that raise themselves, standing densely, some 100ft. or 200ft. over them, are seen in prodigal profusion. As we approach the steep grade, our driver suggests that the gentlemen should walk, a companion and myself take a short cut along a pathway cleared through the frondiferous growth. We are at once in Fairyland; shady dells and bosky bowers present themselves at every turn. Were the messenger of the Fairy Queen to oppose our way and demand a reason for our intrusion, we should not feel at all surprised. His presence there would simply be quite in keeping with the prospect. From the summit of the ascent the road winds round the hill-slope. At every turn fresh exclamations of delight are made, as the wonderful growth and graceful forms of the vegetation reveal fresh beauties. The mountain is long and somewhat narrow. Its north and south ends are capped with a volcanic overflow. About half-way along the hill the Hawkesbury sandstone re-appears, and thus the botanical and geological contrast may be easily seen. There are short leaders on the east and west sides, standing out as bold headlands, with great walls of sandstone having the basaltic formation overlying.

Our friend's hospitable cottage reached, we cannot help pouring out our heartfelt thanks for the pleasure he has given us. He has some seven acres, which, when occupied by him, was densely overgrown with great forest trees, messmate and blackbut and gum, with an almost impenetrable undergrowth of ferns. The cottage is almost wholly built of the timber of a few trees, which stood within a few yards of the present door. All these have been cleared away, and a gentle slope covered with white clover and English grasses, with here and there a clump of tree ferns making shaded arbours, leads down to a fruit garden, where strawberries, raspberries and gooseberries and apples of

almost abnormal size flourish in great perfection.
Roses, phloxes and hydrangeas and countless other
flowering plants add colour and perfume to the little
spot.   We make no explorations that evening, and the
next morning, lo ! and behold the whole place is en-
veloped in a dense mist.   A veritable Scotch mist, not
rain, but with vesicles large enough to wet one through,
and that gathers on the trees' leaves and drops from them
in constant patter, soaking the earth over their roots.
In the afternoon the mist rises, and a company of elders
and young people wander away on a stroll.   At one part
of our walk in the sandstone gap of the hill, on the top
of a great cliff, to look over which will make one giddy,
we discover two couples of lovers of the human species.
An elevation of 3600ft. above the sea, with its chilling
influence, it would seem, has no appreciable effect
in discouraging sweet intercourse of this kind.   An
interesting, but somewhat sad, evidence of former
aboriginal dwellers was seen in the scolloped grooves in
the flat sandstones, where they had sharpened their
stone tomahawks.   We are now treading the soil sacred
to the " Geebung."   This national and somewhat symbolic fruit always reminds me of an old friend, now no
more.   I mean Michael Fitzpatrick.   When the Farnell-
Fitzpatrick Ministry was formed, as it consisted chiefly
of natives of the country, in a moment of rollicking fun,
his sides shaking with laughter, he dubbed it the
" Geebung Government."   Ah well, I wish he were
still amongst us, and may heaven send many more such
"geebungs" to add acrid honesty and shining brightness
to our public life.   He was a man of whom the more
one knew the more one loved and respected.   Full of
an almost boyish lightheartedness, and brimming over
with fun and good humour, he had a great fund of
practical strong common sense, and so honest that even
if he deemed it the wiser policy to act for the public

good against his convictions, he would ·unhesitatingly explain and justify the apparent inconsistency. There was not an atom of intentional deception in him. He was a man who, in considering State affairs, could listen, somewhat uneasily perhaps, to the inconsequential chatter of others working to no practical conclusion, and then, like a sledge-hammer, with one blow settle the whole business. With a kindness of heart that made him one of nature's gentlemen, with keen percep-tions of right and wrong, with a hatred of all trickery, with a knowledge of affairs and an experience gathered largely behind the scenes of public life, with clear expression and polished diction in debate, and much patriotic enthusiasm, the too early death of Michael Fitzpatrick was a great and distinct loss to his country. Pondering thus of my dear old friend so absurdly sug-gested to me, wandering through the great primeval forest (hushed in stillness) of the land he loved so well and with leaden skies overhead, thinking of how much service he might now be in the disturbed condition of our affairs, I returned home filled with a not unpleasing sadness. In the morning the mists had all cleared away, and then we understood the wonderful change in climate that a few thousand feet will make under the same sky. The thermometer had gone down to 53deg. ; the ladies sat round a cheerful fire. This, too, at a time when we learned from the newspapers that the rest of the country was stewing under a heat of from 90deg. to 115deg. in the shade. Under a bright sky and cool air we sally forth to see more of the glories of Mount Wilson, and pursue a northerly direction. From a position on Mr. Wynne's beautiful grounds, and to the north through a cleft in the trees and across the great yawning ravine of the Wallangambe, we look upon a scene of natural desolation, rare even in that region. For miles there is not a foot of land to tempt human settlement. Great gaps are cut through the sandstone rocks, steep and impassable precipices forming their sides—acres of rock without an atom of soil upon them. Stunted trees, however, grow wherever roothold can be found. Between us and the horizon we can see the intervals between the hill tops that mark ravine after ravine, and the Colo, the Wolgan, and far away the Capertee Valleys. Beyond these, mountain peaks appear like small clouds against the sky. Quite near the lovely blue haze—the very despair of painters and from which these mountains have their name—softens the rocks with its transparent ultramarine hue. It is so visible and so impalpable, so sensibly present and so intangible, as though a portion of the farthest sky had descended for very pity to clothe the nakedness of nature with its own diaphanous covering.

We look towards the east, and the valley of the Hawkesbury with the village of Richmond lie plainly visible, some 4000 feet below us. With the aid of field glasses we know a long white streak on the horison to be the city of Sydney. We descend the eastern slope through a small field, in which cocksfoot and red clover grow luxuriantly. This is only obtained by a great expense; forest trees and tree ferns, and vines and small ferns, and great rotting logs innumerable, have to be removed before such an opening can be made, costing not less than £25 per acre. In front of us rises a great wall of forest trees, principally sassafras. The undergrowth is of tree ferns. When we are in it and under it, we find that the leafy covering overhead is so dense that the rays of the sun never reach the earth, which is almost bare of herbage. The surface of the ground is covered with the casts of those monstrous earth-worms, which are more like snakes than the ordinary well-known garden annelid. As we walk along, scrambling over great trunks of trees lying in moist decay, we become filled with a weird feeling, begotten of the silence and the shade. The stillness is suddenly broken by a shrill whistle, followed by a sweeping slash as of an unseen whip. It is as if the evil genius of the place was at length aroused by our presence, and would drive us back. This is the love song of the coachwhip bird, and we recognised him as the proper inhabitant of such horror-haunted woods. For now we feel something gelid crawling up our legs, and hasty examination discloses the fact that numberless leeches find a congenial habitation among the rotting leaves strewn upon the surface. So we make our way out again into the more joyful sunshine. We saw where human beings had apparently slept for the night in this place. Imagination could sup on horrors innumerable, while the leeches innumerable could sup on them. A tree, the "quintinia," quite in keeping with the other terrors of the locality, grows here. It is both parasite and paracide. Its seed takes root on the soft sides of a tree fern, and sends a trunk upwards and a root downwards. We saw two specimens. One was just forming into a tall, thin sapling, springing from the fern's side. The poor fern, all unknowing of the viper it had taken into its bosom, with its fangs fixed upon its heart, looked, I thought, rather admiringly upwards at its destroyer, while it encircled its slender trunk lovingly with its drooping fronds. The other specimen was a large grown tree, still holding to its side the dead remains of its benefactor fern, from which it had sprung and sucked the lifeblood.

From the vigorous and gigantic growth of the vegetation here, it would almost seem as though the spirit of the old volcanic forces that formed the mountain top still exerts its Titanic influence. This place is, I imagine, so unrivalled in New South Wales that I can only hope the day may come when more of the public may be permitted to enjoy its beauties.

It would be a breach of hospitality and of confidence were I to make any suggestions as to how this might be done. I can only appeal to those now in possession to initiate something that will render a more widespread pleasure possible, and hope that a prejudice that sometimes comes of isolation, and is jealous of intrusion, may not be allowed by them to stand in the way.